The Flying

Tim Walker lives with his family in Kent, where he runs a design consultancy from an office set in the grounds of a beautiful country club. *The Flying Fizzler*, his second children's book, is the sequel to *Shipley Manor*.

Praise for *Shipley Manor*:

'This is a lively read, with more than enough fantastical inventions and thrilling cliffhangers to keep children turning the pages; just don't expect impressionable readers ever to settle for a proper job in future.' *Financial Times*

'An impressively fluent debut, with colourful, larger-than-life characters – very good read aloud material.' *Times Educational Supplement*

'An action-packed fantasy adventure story that should appeal to fans of Roald Dahl . . . Filled with humour, invention and larger-than-life characters.' *Bertrams Books*

'It's a magical story laced with reality that works for both adults and children – certainly one to be enjoyed reading together.' *Irish Times*

'*Shipley Manor* is a fantastic read packed full of imagination in creating a wonderful and bizarre fantasy world.' *Write Away*

'A pacey story full of laughs and excitement.' *Primary Times*

faber and faber

First published in 2008
by Faber and Faber Limited
3 Queen Square London WC1N 3AU

Typeset by Faber and Faber
Printed in England by
CPI BookMarque, Croydon

A CIP record for this book
is available from the British Library

ISBN 978–0–571–23301–4

2 4 6 8 10 9 7 5 3 1

To Audrey and Denis Walker

1918

Tom was almost over the battlefield now. He popped another toffee into his mouth and lifted his battle-scarred biplane through the frost-bitten night sky, levelling out above range of the enemy machine guns which he knew would be there to greet him. Despite a scattering of dark clouds, the peek-a-boo moon cast a crisp blue light over the ground – perfect conditions for him to observe the movement of enemy troops. He shouted over his shoulder to the empty seat behind him, 'Ears pricked, eyes sharp, Archie!' But he knew there was no one there. Bitterly he looked down at the line of bullet holes which stretched across the canvas wings, a gut-wrenching reminder of the fierce aerial battle that morning in which his beloved brother had been killed, leaving him to fly tonight's observation mission alone.

Suddenly the landscape changed. Instead of dark-green forest there was nothing below him now except a wasteland of festering brown sludge. Across it, two parallel trenches stretched like infected scars, oozing poisonous gas and columns of damp, acrid shell-smoke into the air as the opposing sides tried to obliterate each other. Tom dug out his observation book, but no sooner had he begun making notes than a raindrop plopped on to the page, smudging the ink. Quickly it was followed by another. Then another. He looked up. A huge black storm-cloud had crept up on him. As it burst open, freezing rain began to batter down on his plane, saturating its wings and pushing him lower and lower towards the enemy guns. Tom turned towards the only patch of clear sky he could see. It was deep inside enemy territory but perhaps, if he reached it, he could regain height and find a way home. As he roared over the enemy trench every machine gun along it stuttered into life, sending up a wall of sizzling hot metal which Tom was too low to escape. As hundreds of bullets sliced through his plane something hit him hard in the chest. He doubled up, gasping, but continued on straight until the mud below him turned back into forest, and the firing stopped.

Still he was far from safe. Fuel was spurting in long liquorice streaks from holes punched in the fuel tanks. He would have to land quickly, before it ran out. He took off his oil-spattered flying goggles and scanned the horizon. Far in the distance he spotted a cluster of lakes twinkling in the moonlight. The nearest seemed to sparkle more brightly than the others, as though it were beckoning him, so Tom pushed the joystick forward and headed towards it. He almost reached it, but as he prepared to land, his engine finally spluttered to a halt and his plane began to sink, silently, into the tree tops. Then, as it passed between two towering pine trees on the water's edge, its wings snapped off like dry twigs, and what remained of the plane, with Tom still strapped inside it, spiralled into the lake. Upside down and with the dark, ice-cold water swirling all around him, Tom pressed the buckle on his seat harness. But it didn't release him. The bullet embedded in it, determined to kill him one way or another, had jammed it shut. As the heavy engine dragged his plane gurgling to the bottom of the lake, Tom's last thought was of the water that was about to consume him. There was something strange about it. And then he realised what it was.

It made his tongue tingle.

An Invitation

Captain Horatio Shipley and his crew invite Tom Sterling to accompany them on the maiden voyage of Shipley Manor – the world's first floating country house. Destination unknown.

'Wake up, Tom. Wake up!'

Tom opened his eyes. He was alone in his bedroom. The girl's voice was in his head.

'Polly?' he replied, silently.

'Of course it's me, sleepy-head. Who else can you talk to like this without anyone else hearing?'

'I've just had such a horrible dream, Polly. I was a First World War pilot and . . .'

'Never mind that now, Tom – have you forgotten

what day it is?'

Tom looked over to the invitation propped up on his dressing table.

'No, of course not,' he replied. 'It's just that the dream was so real, Polly. My plane crashed and . . .'

'Well, hurry up then – your train leaves in an hour.'

Tom's father Roger called to him from the bottom of the stairs.

'Breakfast is on the table, Tom.'

'Thanks, Dad,' Tom called back.

He jumped out of bed. Polly was right – he needed to get a move on.

'I have to go,' he told her. 'See you aboard ship!'

An hour later Tom boarded his train and swung his neatly packed rucksack on to an overhead rack. There were plenty of spare seats, so he chose one next to the platform so that he could wave goodbye to his father. Roger had been invited to spend the summer aboard Shipley Manor too, but had felt duty-bound to stay behind. Since becoming manager of Shipley Bank he had discovered that his crooked, highly pungent predecessor, Barclay Grub – now securely behind bars in Shipley Prison – had stolen a fortune from it. Although Grub refused to say where it was hidden, Roger was determined to find every penny. Until he did, a holiday was out of the question.

A shrill whistle pierced the air and the train jerked forwards. Tom was on his way. He waved until his father became a dot on the platform, then settled back in his seat to enjoy the journey to the naval dockyard. Shipley Manor had been moored there for a month now, ever since the magic water – the Fizzle, as its residents called it – had ripped the house out of the ground and carried it down to the sea. Tom had seen photographs of it in the newspaper, dwarfed between two huge oil tankers which were moored either side of it. Although the Fizzle had protected the house on its bone-shaking journey and seemed content to remain around and under it like a vast liquid mattress, the Captain knew it might not protect them for ever. So, using the treadmills as paddles he had sailed Shipley Manor to the nearest dockyard where it could be made properly seaworthy – 'shipshape', as he called it. The improvement work was now complete, and although Polly and Tom hadn't met during this time they had spoken to each other every day. But not on the phone. They had discovered that, unlike their shipmates who had only ever drunk the Fizzle, breathing the gas contained in its tiny bubbles had given them a special connection, allowing them to talk to each other no matter how far apart they were. Their conversations took place silently, inside their heads, one of them thinking the words, the other hearing them. So far they hadn't told anyone what they could do: Tom because he was worried that people wouldn't believe him and Polly because she wanted to play a few tricks on her shipmates first, especially Seymour.

By now the train had left the houses and factories behind it and was rattling through the English countryside towards the coast. Gazing out of the window, Tom spotted a small private aircraft flying parallel to his carriage. From a distance the pilot appeared to be wearing an old-fashioned leather flying hat, much like the one he'd worn in his dream. The pilot saw Tom looking and waved, before tipping the plane's wings and veering away towards the horizon. Watching it turn, Tom recalled his dream from the night before and felt a sudden sick, empty feeling swirl around his stomach and up into his throat. 'Oh Archie,' he moaned, loud enough for several of his fellow passengers to look up from their newspapers. He hugged his stomach and flopped weakly against the side of the carriage. He knew perfectly well that a dream was only a dream and that he didn't have a brother called Archie. Yet he felt so wretched. Surely he couldn't be missing his father already, could he? He'd only just said goodbye to him.

At last the train reached its destination and Tom's thoughts returned to Shipley Manor. He caught a taxi to the docks and ten minutes later found himself standing on the quayside looking up at the familiar old house. It was moored facing out to sea, with the drawbridge at the rear of the building connecting it to the quayside. At first glance only the treadmills on either side of the drawbridge seemed to have changed. They were proper paddle-wheels now, their inner walkways having been replaced by powerful wooden blades which cut deep into the water, ready to push Shipley Manor through it fast. Tom looked over the edge of the quay and smiled at the sparkling Fizzle as though it were an old friend. The last time he had seen the water it had unleashed itself in a terrifying display of force. Now it lay dormant again, its soft, whispering hiss concealing its true power, like the gentle ticking of a bomb.

Tom caught a brightly coloured reflection in the water and looked up. Polly was standing on the drawbridge. She was wearing a Hawaiian hula-hula dancer's raffia skirt, a bikini top made from two coconut shells and, around her neck, dozens of tissue-paper flowers draped in a ragged rainbow of multi-coloured garlands. But it was her hair that drew Tom's attention. Sparkling sea-blue, it curved upwards from the back of her head like a single, high-rolling wave, before tipping over at the top and cascading back towards her forehead in a froth of foamy white curls.

'All you need is a surfer riding on top,' said Tom.

'I'm still making that,' Polly replied, spinning around and rustling the skirt with her fingers.

'So . . . can you guess where we're going?'

Tom laughed, then rubbed his chin, frowning.

'Mmmm, that's a difficult one. Let me think . . . Hawaii?'

'Wrong!' she replied gleefully. 'You're so easy to trick, Tom.'

She grabbed his hand. 'Come on, I've got lots to show you.'

Much to his embarrassment, Polly forced Tom to hula-dance with her over the drawbridge and into the kitchen, where his shipmates – the Captain, Slugbucket, Seymour and Maggie, Polly's mother – had gathered around the table to greet him. Maggie was busy trying to coax a spoonful of porridge past the stubborn lips of Polly's baby sister Calypso, who was sitting in her high chair facing the door. She gasped with delight when she saw Tom, only to find her mouth suddenly filled with porridge.

'Welcome aboard, shipmate,' the Captain boomed, leaping to his feet. He shook Tom's hand vigorously before leading him to the table. 'I hope you still like carrot cake,' he said, handing him a huge slice.

Tom sat down between Calypso and Polly – who, to her mother's disapproval, had already begun tucking into hers – and nibbled politely as the Captain brought him up to date with developments. Edna and Constance wouldn't be joining them on their voyage, he was told. Constance had decided that she was too old for such adventures and Edna, who suffered from seasickness anyway, had offered to stay behind in Shipley to look after her. Apart from that, the crew was all set to go. Except, of course, that they hadn't yet managed to agree on a destination.

'Perhaps you can help us decide,' the Captain told him. 'It's high tide tomorrow, so we'll be leaving for a couple of days' sea trials. After that we can go anywhere. And while you're thinking about it you can learn what everything on board is called. Shipley Manor is officially a ship now, Tom, so we're going to treat her like one. From now on the kitchen will be called the galley, the conservatory will be known as the bridge and you will be sleeping on a bunk in your cabin. There'll be no more of that landlubbing "bedroom" nonsense.'

'Aye, aye, Captain,' Tom replied, entering into the nautical spirit.

'Galloping guppies, he's got it,' the Captain laughed. 'Polly can teach you the rest whilst she's showing you around. We've made quite a few changes to the place. Have you spotted any of them yet?'

'You've turned the treadmills into paddle-wheels.'

The Captain looked disappointed.

'Anything else, perhaps?' he said, leaning closer.

Then Tom realised. The answer was staring him in the face.

'You've changed your beard,' he said. 'It's in the shape of Africa.'

The Captain slapped the table.

'Well spotted, young man. South America was growing so overcrowded that I thought I'd try a bigger continent. The principle's the same, though. I keep my keys in Kenya, sunglasses in Sudan, a tasty nibble or two in Nigeria. Besides, Polly thinks Africa makes me look more . . . mysterious, don't you, Polly?'

She nodded, pushing the last piece of cake into her mouth. She was raring to go, so as soon as Tom had cleared his plate she hurried him upstairs to drop his rucksack off in his cabin – which was next to hers – and then took him up on to the roof, or, as the Captain insisted on calling it now, the top deck.

Unlike the rest of the building, which had remained largely unchanged, the flat roof had been transformed. Now it was a garden, with a single woodchip path stretching full circle around it, weaving its way among the numerous curved flower beds and vegetable patches like a river meandering through a network of lakes. Dotted along the route was an assortment of water barrels, Maggie's home-made earthenware pots, overflowing with colourful summer plants, and garden seats constructed from passing driftwood. Several of Slugbucket's giant carvings – the proud sea-horses, leaping dolphins and fearsome sea-dragons which he'd spent years creating from uprooted tree-trunks on the Shipley Manor estate – had also survived the journey down to the sea. Having been plucked out of the water, they now stood sentry among the vegetables, warding off hungry seagulls. Towards the rear of the house two wind turbines, each almost as high as the Crow's Nest – the stone tower which rose up from the courtyard in the centre of the building – had been installed to help power the paddle-wheels directly below them. Even in the light breeze, Tom noticed that their blades were turning with a low hum, storing up energy for the voyage to come. Between them hung a washing line, on which an assortment of Polly's outfits were flapping gently in the wind.

‘Another energy-generating device?’ Tom asked, jokingly.

‘How did you guess?’ Polly replied. ‘Whenever we need some extra sail-power we just hang a few pairs of Slugbucket’s enormous underpants up there.’

Tom laughed, and looked over to the gypsy caravan which stood a few metres away. Although Slugbucket still slept in it, Tom noticed that it was hooked up to a winch which, in an emergency, could lift it up and lower it over the side like a lifeboat. Nautipus, Slugbucket’s fluffy white cat, was asleep on the top step. Some things never change, thought Tom.

He and Polly continued along the path until they reached the conservatory at the other end of the house. Tom noticed that now it had a red roof. Polly explained that as they could no longer take walks inside the treadmills to generate power for the house, the conservatory roof had been covered with solar panels that would trap the sun’s rays and convert them into electricity. Minor changes had been made inside, too. The ship’s wheel stood proudly looking out to sea just as Tom remembered it, but Seymour had found a way to connect it directly to the paddle-wheels, so that the Captain could steer Shipley Manor as though it were any normal ship. A lever rising from the floor to the left of the wheel controlled Shipley Manor's speed, whilst another lever marked 'Forward-Neutral-Reverse' was situated on the opposite side.

'What happened to the controls in the cellar – I mean the "engine room"?' asked Tom.

'They're all gone,' Polly explained. 'The Captain cleared out the cellar and pumped it full of high-buoyancy foam. He said that if ever the Fizzle decided to leave us we'd need to be able to stay afloat on ordinary seawater.'

Tom nodded approvingly. Very sensible.

'That's why he and Seymour added fins to the house as well.'

Fins? Tom hadn't noticed those, so Polly led him to the edge of the roof and leaned over the wall.

'Down there,' she said, pointing.

Sure enough, a row of fins each the size of a table-tennis table protruded from the side of the building, rocking back and forth on top of the gently undulating water.

'They work like the stabilisers I used to have on the back of my bicycle,' Polly explained, 'to stop the house tipping over sideways in a storm. They make electricity too – every time a wave makes them rock up and down.' As she spoke a brightly coloured Fizzlefish, which Tom recognised as a Neon Rainbow Fish, leapt out of the water and flew over one of the giant fins.

'The Fizzlefish came with us,' she explained. 'I've pulled every one of them out of the water with my Fizzlestick and oiled their hinges so they can keep up with us when we leave. Catching them was easy from the drawbridge. That's my favourite place now. So long as the sea's not too rough we can lower it to fish from, or use it as a diving platform, or have picnics on it, all with the water lapping just a few inches below us.'

Tom looked over the side again. The fins reminded him of something else. Aeroplane wings. Suddenly his thoughts returned to Archie – the brother he knew he didn't really have – and the same hollow ache crept back into his stomach. Perhaps it was nothing more than seasickness. Either way the thought of food made him feel quite ill, so he told Polly that he would have to skip lunch and asked her to make his apologies to the others. Then, feeling utterly miserable, he trudged alone to his cabin. Perhaps he would feel better once he'd had a rest. So, after he'd unpacked his rucksack and hung his dressing gown neatly on the back of his cabin door, he curled up on the bunk clutching his tummy, and closed his eyes.

He hadn't meant to fall asleep. But the next thing he knew he was trapped once again in what remained of his biplane, spiralling towards the bottom of an icy-cold lake. Streams of silvery bubbles were making their own bid for freedom through the numerous bullet holes which peppered the side of the fuselage. But there was no such escape for him. As the bubbles fled past his face on their way to the surface, he tried to catch some in his mouth, to take what he feared would be his last breath. But as he opened his mouth the plane hit the bottom and Tom's head struck the windscreen in front of him. When he regained consciousness a few seconds later he found, to his amazement, that a large bubble had formed around him, allowing him to breathe. Stranger still, someone was tapping him on the shoulder. He turned around nervously. Behind him was a young man, wearing an identical flying suit to his own.

'I say, old chap,' said the young man, slowly chewing on a toffee, 'I rather think you're sitting in my seat.'

Mind-manners

Tom sat up in his bunk and fumbled for the light. He was alone, but he could still hear the pilot talking to him.

'I hope you've got a jolly good reason to be rummaging about inside my head, young man.'

Tom looked around his cabin again, uncertain what to do next.

Perhaps he should reply – silently, as though he were speaking secretly to Polly.

'Are you . . . talking to me?' he asked, nervously.

'Well, it's high time somebody did,' replied the voice. 'You can't go around helping yourself to other people's memories like that. It's like breaking into their house and reading their diary.'

'I'm so sorry,' Tom explained. 'I thought I was

just . . . dreaming.'

The voice softened.

'Well, it might have been a dream to you, my dear fellow. But that was my plane, and my crash, and Archie . . . was my brother.'

Now Tom understood. It wasn't his own misery that he'd been feeling all day. It was the pilot's.

'I'm so sorry,' he said again. Then he realised something else.

'But . . . the First World War was so long ago – that means you must be . . .'

'A hundred and six years old, that's right. Or maybe I'm a hundred and seven, I can never remember. You tend to lose count after the first hundred years.'

'You don't sound a hundred and six,' observed Tom.

'I expect that's because the words aren't coming out of my wrinkled old mouth,' replied the voice, 'at least not as far as I can help it. I'm just thinking them, the same as you. Anyway, where are my manners? Let me introduce myself. Squadron Leader Harry Hawkins at your service. You can call me "Hopper" if you like. Everyone does. Never got the hang of landing my plane properly, you see. I could do everything else: loop the loops, barrel rolls, flying upside down – I even tried a spot of wing-walking once – but, for some reason, whenever I came in to land my plane would hop along the runway like a demented kangaroo with its tail on fire. Frightfully embarrassing for a squadron leader, I can tell you.'

'Pleased to meet you,' said Tom. 'My name's Tom Sterling.'

'I know,' replied Hopper, much to Tom's surprise, 'and perhaps it's I who should apologise. About a month ago I began to hear you and Polly talking to each other. I had no idea who you were, or where your voices were coming from. I assumed they were coming from the room next door to mine, or from a radio left on somewhere. When it turned out to be neither, I decided that my mind had finally begun to play tricks on me. But then I heard you talking about the magic water you call 'Fizzle', and how the bubbles had gathered together and allowed you both to breathe under water. Suddenly I realised that the three of us – you, me and Polly – had accidentally become members of a very exclusive club. All three of us have breathed in the Fizzle gas and now we have this special connection to each other. I haven't listened to any of your conversations since then, of course. That would never do.'

'Thank you,' said Tom. 'But how did you stop yourself from overhearing us?'

'That turned out to be easy,' Hopper replied. 'I

imagined that my ear was pressed up against a wall so that I could hear you on the other side. Then I simply took my ear away. It's a shame you're not really next door – I've been waiting a very long time to meet someone else like me.'

'Where are you?' asked Tom.

'In the Skyview Nursing Home . . .' replied Hopper. 'In America.'

'America!' Tom gasped. 'That's over three thousand miles away!'

'I told you our connection was special. I would have contacted you sooner but I've been rather ill. Even now I'm lying flat on my back with more tubes coming out of me than a toothpaste factory. The one consolation is that my room overlooks an airfield, so I can watch the planes come and go. That was my great granddaughter Scarlett's idea. She's a flyer like me, you see, never happier than when she's up in the clouds getting into trouble. She even has the same curly red hair I had when I was her age – without the moustache, of course.'

Hopper fell silent for a moment.

'Is something wrong?' asked Tom.

'My nurse is looking at me very oddly,' Hopper continued, cautiously. 'I know I should be able to talk to you without moving my lips, but I'm so old I can't stop them trembling. I'm sure she thinks I've finally gone bonkers and started talking to myself. I can hardly tell her that I'm talking to you, though, can I?' Suddenly he exploded into laughter. 'Of course, I may not be talking to you at all – have you considered that, Tom?' Hopper's laugh stumbled into a bubbly cough as he tried to complete his joke.

' . . . In which case, you're the one . . .' He coughed then tried again: '. . . you're the one who's bonkers!'

Tom laughed out loud, then wondered whether anyone in the house had heard him.

'What happened after you woke up at the bottom of the lake?' he continued.

'Well, I realised that anything was possible, of course. Not only had a huge bubble formed around me, allowing me to breathe, but the plane's windscreen had smashed, scattering jagged pieces of glass all over the cockpit. I used one of them to cut through the straps on my seat harness.'

'Then you swam to the surface?' asked Tom.

'No, I wanted to taste the water properly this time, so I pressed my lips up against the outside of the bubble and sucked in another mouthful. I'm sure you can guess what happened next.'

'You "Got the Fizzle"?'

'That's right. Suddenly, I felt connected to everything – to the Fizzle itself, to the fish who swim in it, the birds who drink it, the plants and trees which suck it up from the ground, the air into which it evaporates and finally, everyone who breathes that air as it circles the earth. The enemy soldiers, who I knew would be searching for me, weren't my enemies at all. They were just part of that one enormous family – my family. That's when I knew what I had to do.'

'What was that?' asked Tom.

'I had to persuade them to drink it, of course. If it made them feel the same as me, they wouldn't want to fight any more. If I could get everyone in the world to drink it, there would be no more wars. No one would ever have to lose a brother again, like I lost poor Archie. I vowed, there and then, that even if it took me the rest of my life, I would make sure that everyone in the world "Got the Fizzle". So I kicked off from my seat and swam up.'

'Were the soldiers waiting for you?' asked Tom.

'They were some distance away, shining their torches into the bushes with their backs to me. I could have escaped, but I was desperate for them to taste the water. So I called out to them.'

'Were they surprised?'

'Oh, they were surprised all right – so surprised they started shooting at me,' Hopper chuckled. 'I threw myself headlong into the nearest patch of long grass and when I looked up a few seconds later they were right in front of me, jerking their rifles and screaming at me to get on my feet. If only I'd been able to speak their language I could have explained about the Fizzle. Instead, I just kept pointing to the water, cupping my frozen hands as if to drink it and trying to hug them like long-lost brothers. I'm sure they thought I'd hit my head too hard on the side of my cockpit or something, especially when I waded back into the freezing-cold water and started scooping up Fizzle in my hands to offer them. Of course it was hopeless. They weren't about to drink water from a lake just because a grinning fool of an Englishman wanted them to. They blindfolded me and shoved me, shivering and wet, into the back of a lorry with twenty other prisoners. Two hours later we were in a prison camp.

'I wasn't to be defeated, though, Tom. I was determined to find that lake again. I thought that if I could fill up a few bottles with the Fizzle and persuade the generals and the politicians on both sides to drink it, they'd stop the fighting. I had to try. Six times I escaped, and six times I was recaptured, usually within a few miles of the prison camp. But on my seventh attempt I found my way back to the lakes, only to discover that there were hundreds of them, covering an area the size of a small country. Worst of all, each one looked much the same as the next.'

'Did you give up?' asked Tom.

'Give up? Hopper Hawkins doesn't give up! I stayed hidden in the forest for a year, eating berries and anything else I could find whilst I travelled from lake to lake, each time hoping the next one would be filled with Fizzle instead of plain water. But it never was. Eventually my own side found me, wandering around like a scarecrow with a beard down to my waist, and told me that the war was over. But I knew there would be more wars, Tom, so even though I moved to America to fly crop-spraying planes, I returned to the lakes every year on holiday to continue my search. I had the crazy idea that if ever I found the Fizzle again I could fill up the tanks of my crop-sprayer and rain it down wherever people were fighting each other. But it wasn't to be. On my last visit I arrived to find that a dam had been built and the whole area had been flooded to become one huge reservoir. Most of the lakes had disappeared. I tasted the water from the reservoir, of course, hoping that it might be the Fizzle. But it wasn't.'

Hopper reflected on his disappointment for a moment, then continued.

'So I decided to look elsewhere. I discovered that some of the lakes had been sitting in the craters of extinct volcanoes. I wondered whether the Fizzle originated underground, and that sometimes it escaped through the same cracks in the earth's crust through which molten lava had once exploded to create the volcanoes themselves.'

'But there aren't any volcanoes where I live,' observed Tom.

'No, but there are cracks in the earth's crust, Tom – ancient fault lines stretching through Shipley right down to the sea. When I read in the newspaper what had happened to Shipley Manor, I asked Scarlett to check for me.'

'Did you ever find the Fizzle?' Tom asked.

'Not a drop. But I had a wonderful time looking. I travelled the world, Tom, following the earth's fault lines across every continent, flying my crop-sprayer around America, dropping food supplies in Africa. I even spent five years travelling around China with my own Flying Circus – you should see my upside-down triple barrel roll. And along the way I landed beside every lake, pond, puddle and waterhole I came across. I must have tasted enough murky water over the years to fill a swimming pool. But I never found what I was looking for. Then, one day I stopped flying. Too old, you see – time to hang up my goggles.'

Hopper paused, but only briefly.

'So then I had another idea.'

Tom laughed. Somehow he'd known that wasn't going to be the end of the story.

'I thought the Fizzle itself might be able to tell me. I had drunk it and breathed it, and could feel that it was still part of me. I knew also that all Fizzle was connected, so perhaps the Fizzle inside me could tell me where the rest of it was. So one day I closed my eyes and tried to look inside my own head to discover the answer.'

'Did you find it?' asked Tom.

'No,' Hopper replied, 'but I did discover that my mind was a fabulous place to visit. Our minds are much like houses, Tom, except that they come in many more shapes and sizes, just like us. Inside there are different rooms in which we keep different things. I have a room where my idle thoughts drift around like wispy clouds, constantly changing shape. Another stuffed to the ceiling with useless bits of information which I only ever dig out when I'm taking part in a quiz. Other rooms in which I keep my most precious memories. Nothing is ever lost, Tom. A perfect record of everything I ever heard, or felt, or saw, or did, or learned is tucked away in one of those rooms.'

'Do you think we might be able to visit each other's minds as though they were real houses?' asked Tom.

'It looks that way,' Hopper replied. 'You've already managed to stumble into one of my memories, haven't you? Perhaps it's time we

"Fizzlers" established a few visiting rules – what do you think?'

Tom liked that idea. He'd been brought up always to obey the rules. It was quite a relief to find that Hopper appreciated the need for them, too.

'We could call them "mind-manners",' he suggested.

'Perfect,' said Hopper. 'So, let me see . . . Rule number one: we must never enter each other's minds uninvited. We must always knock on the door first, just as we would if we were visiting a real house.'

'How do we do that?' asked Tom.

'Your guess is as good as mine, Tom. Maybe we just imagine knocking, or think the words "Knock knock". I'm sure we'll find a way. Rule number two: once inside, we behave as house guests should. Feet off the furniture, and no wandering into rooms that are clearly private. We all have a right to keep some things secret.'

'Like what we've bought each other for our birthdays,' Tom suggested.

'Exactly,' Hopper agreed. 'Rule number three: when asked to leave, we do so straightaway.'

'Of course,' agreed Tom.

'And finally,' Hopper continued, 'rule number four: when we do leave, we never take anything that doesn't belong to us.'

Tom was shocked by the mere suggestion.

'Oh, I'd never do anything like that,' he assured Hopper. 'But . . . does that mean there are things in your mind which I could steal?'

'It's more like illegal copying really, but yes, there are, especially in the basement where I keep all the skills I've learned over the years, like how to lasso cattle and fly aeroplanes upside down.'

'Does that mean I could learn to fly?' asked Tom, excitedly.

'That's the thing. You wouldn't have to learn, Tom, you'd just be able to do it. That is, of course, if I let you take that particular skill away, which I won't do just yet. Learning to fly took me a lot of time and effort and I'm not about to pass on that skill without good reason. I can let you have my lassoing skills, though. Perhaps you should pay my mind a visit now. We have to try it sooner or later.'

'I don't know how to,' Tom replied. 'I can hear your voice but I can't see anything except my cabin.'

'Then close your eyes, Tom, and start counting backwards from ten. At the same time, imagine yourself flying over rooftops. Keep looking down at them as they drift underneath you, and wait for one of them to draw you to it. When you find the right place, don't bother to knock this time – just let yourself in.'

Hopper's Last Request

Tom lay back on his pillow and closed his eyes. Darkness. He began counting backwards, picturing the rooftops of Shipley, which he'd observed many times whilst flying his kite from a nearby hillside. As an image of them formed inside his head, he imagined being the kite, suddenly cut free from the line holding it to the ground. Dipping his head, he swooped down, allowing the wind to carry him straight and level as the rooftops passed underneath him. He could see them clearly now, growing in number and variety far beyond anything he'd ever seen in Shipley. But which one belonged to Hopper? How could he tell? Should he be looking for the oldest house, or might Hopper have left a sign, like a big 'X' on the lawn? Perhaps he had. In the distance Tom saw a windsock flying from a tall white pole. He had seen one before at the side of an airfield, stretched tight in the wind like a fluorescent orange tunnel. It had to belong to Hopper. He flew closer. The windsock was situated in a garden, but where Hopper's house should have been there was nothing but bare earth. What had Hopper said? Don't bother to knock. But how could he knock if there was no door? Then he realised: the windsock was the door. He flattened his arms against his sides and flew into its open mouth. To his surprise he didn't emerge on the other side straightaway. Instead, the tunnel continued, twisting and turning as the wind buffeted its thin fabric walls, before coughing him out several seconds later into what looked like an aircraft hangar. To Tom's delight the air inside was full of Fizzle bubbles. With no breeze to support him now, Tom sank slowly to the concrete floor below, the bubbles gently pushed aside by the draught of his descent.

Landing softly on his feet next to Hopper's biplane, he ran his hand over the wing nearest him, feeling a mixture of anger and sadness as his fingers dipped into the bullet holes. Then he looked up. The hangar was very high, its skylit roof curving gracefully to meet the rooms which extended over several floors around three of its sides, connected by a network of iron staircases and walkways. On the fourth side – the end nearest Tom – a pair of giant sliding doors sat beneath a semi-circular window. From it, a single blade of light cut a diagonal line through the hangar to a door at the other end, causing the bubbles passing through it to flash brightly. Tom began to weave his way through the other planes on the hangar floor – crop-sprayers, assorted seaplanes and, beyond them, a flame-red biplane with a Chinese dragon and 'Hopper Hawkins' Flying Circus' painted on its side. This plane wasn't resting on the ground like the others. To Tom's amazement it hung in the air, spinning slowly in a perpetual, gravity-defying barrel roll, its wings threatening to clip his head as he ducked underneath.

At last he reached the side of the hangar and could walk freely around the perimeter, towards the doorway illuminated at the other end. On the way he passed numerous other doors, some of which had small windows set into them. Those that didn't Tom presumed to be private, containing thoughts and memories that Hopper didn't wish to share, or perhaps even to visit himself. From one he could hear the sound of frightened shouts and stuttering machine-gun fire, of explosions and spattered earth, as though a fierce battle were raging inside. From another a low moaning, as though someone inside were dying. Tom put his hand to his stomach. No wonder Hopper wanted to keep some things locked away. Those doors with windows he was happy to peer into. Through one he saw a red setting sun sinking slowly into a vast expanse of ocean. He looked down at his feet, almost expecting to find water seeping out from under the door, but of course it wasn't. The ocean was simply a memory. The next door boasted a small brass sign attached to it just below the window: 'Mission HQ' it read. He tried the handle. It was unlocked. Perhaps Hopper was inviting him to enter. Tom stepped inside.

At first the room appeared to be empty, its bare walls, floor and ceiling painted a dull, lifeless grey. But in the centre Tom saw a single glass sphere, about the size of a basketball, rotating slowly in mid-air. As he drew closer he saw that it was a globe, but unlike the one in his bedroom at home, neither land nor sea was marked on it. Instead, it showed the web of fractures and fault lines in the earth's crust underneath, and marked every point at which these cracks reached the surface – the volcanoes, geysers and hot springs – that were connected to each other around the world regardless of national boundaries. Each of them, from the volcanic crater lakes in Germany to the hot springs of Wyoming, was marked by its place name. Tom took the globe and began turning it slowly in his hands. Then he found what he was looking for: Shipley.

The second his eyes focused on the small red dot marking his home town, the walls, the ceiling, the floor – even the air around him – came alive. Suddenly the room was filled with maps of Shipley Estate, geological drawings, rotating three-dimensional diagrams, television and newspaper clippings about Shipley Manor and the 'magic' water that had uprooted it and carried it down to the sea. As he turned the globe, looking from place to place, so an endless succession of new maps and charts presented themselves, along with newspaper cuttings going back hundreds of years, and historical documents describing the 'magic' water dating back even further. Tom watched respectfully as the vast library of information – Hopper's life's work – flashed around him, stopping occasionally to examine an item in detail. Some of it he didn't understand. But one thing seemed clear. Even though the Fizzle had risen to the surface in different countries, and at different times, its underground reservoirs were all connected, joined through cracks deep in the earth's crust, like cities linked by a network of roads. Finally, Tom let go of the globe and it resumed its position, quietly rotating in the middle of the room just as he'd found it. He closed the door behind him and continued on.

The door at the end of the hangar was still bathed in a bright, beckoning light. When he reached it the door swung open for him, and he descended a set of steep wooden steps to the basement below. Although it was dark, the room seemed to be no wider than his outstretched arms. He flipped a switch by his elbow and strip lights in the arched ceiling flickered on one by one, pushing the room out in front of him, like an endless corridor with no doors. A wooden shelf ran the full length of one side, upon which stood thousands of sweet-jars, each one labelled. The first jar was filled with clear boiled sweets shaped like teardrops, and read 'Crying'. The first thing Hopper learned to do when he was born, thought Tom. Perhaps the jars were in order. Sure enough, he soon came upon one brimming with gold chocolate coins marked 'Counting' and shortly after that, another full of foil-covered chocolate footballs marked 'Playing soccer'. He looked up. The end of the room was still no more than a dot, so he quickened his pace. Perhaps he would find a 'Lassoing' jar. He found it several minutes later sandwiched between 'Flying' and 'Rock climbing' but decided to continue to the end, just to see what else Hopper had learned to do in his eventful life. It was a long walk: 'Swimming', 'Tunnelling', 'Escapology' (which was empty, much to Tom's amusement), 'Fencing', 'Wing-walking', 'Aerobatics', 'Chinese finger-fighting', 'Volcanology', a jar full of bonbons labelled 'Speaking French' – the jars seemed to go on for ever. Finally, though, after almost an hour he reached the last one, a jar of dimpled white gobstoppers labelled 'Playing Golf', so he turned round and trotted back to the 'Lassoing' jar. It appeared to be full of liquorice bootlaces plaited together like rope. What should he do now?

'Eat one.'

Tom jumped, almost knocking the jar over. He turned to find a young-looking Hopper Hawkins sitting on the basement steps, dressed in the same flying suit and oil-spattered flying hat that he'd been wearing in Tom's dream. Hopper's rust-red moustache was see-sawing gently up and down as he chewed a toffee.

'You have to consume the knowledge, you see, Tom,' he explained slowly. 'Absorb it, just as you do when you learn anything. Only this is quicker. Normally you have to read something, don't you, or listen to something, or watch how something works before you can do it yourself. But this way the learning is instant, because the knowledge is contained in a single sweet that you can eat. The moment it's inside you it becomes part of you, and it's yours.'

'Does it only work with sweets?' asked Tom.

'Oh no, I chose sweets because I happen to have a sweet tooth. I could just as easily fill the jars with fruit juices that could be drunk, or smells that could be sniffed, or I could make everything I've learned almost impossible to steal by filling the jars with live scorpions, or boiling acid. But I saw so many horrible sights during the war, Tom, I only want to fill my head with nice things now. So go ahead, help yourself.'

Tom unscrewed the lid and took a bootlace out of the jar. He sniffed it, nervously.

'Don't worry, you won't taste anything much,' Hopper reassured him. 'There's no real satisfaction in learning this way, you see. It's too easy, like passing an exam when the answers have already been filled in for you. Proper learning should be like chewing this toffee, Tom – a slow . . . delicious pleasure, full of . . . flavour.' He leaned back, propping his elbows on the dusty wooden step behind him.

'Don't take too long, though, old chap. I may be a hundred and six years old but I still have things to do.'

Tom tipped his head back and lowered the liquorice into his mouth. Hopper was right, it barely tasted of anything. But it certainly had plenty of fizz. At first the fizz filled his mouth, making his gums tingle. Then it whooshed around his body and down his arms and legs, before shooting back upwards and finally, with the biggest tingle of all, bursting into his head. It wasn't a particularly pleasant feeling like a shiver or a sneeze. It was more like having a cold, tickly shower – on the inside.

'Now picture your cabin, Tom, and open your eyes.'

Tom opened his eyes and found himself back in his cabin. He leaped out of his bunk and unhooked his dressing gown from the cabin door. Quickly he unthreaded the cord and, as though his fingers had done it a thousand times, tied a perfect slipknot in the end to make a loop. Then he stepped back from the door and spun the loop above his head before launching it at the doorknob. He scored a direct hit. The loop slipped over the doorknob and with an instinctive flick of his wrist he pulled it tight. Another flick and it was free. He wound the cord back in and repeated the experiment successfully. There was no doubt about it.

'It worked, Hopper, it worked!'

'That's good,' Hopper replied, 'because there's something I want to ask you – my last request, you might say.'

Tom sat back on his bunk. Hopper's voice continued sombrely.

'As you know, I've spent most of my life searching for the Fizzle, but it's always eluded me. Instead, it found you and your friend Polly. That's why I want you to complete my mission for me, Tom. I want you to find a way to share that Fizzle around the world. If you agree, you can have any skill I've learned over the past hundred and six years – whatever you need.'

Tom's mind filled with doubts. He had never been one to avoid taking responsibility, but no one had ever asked him to do anything so important before. And what about the 'never-make-promises-you-can't-keep' rule his father had taught him? He didn't want to break that. He found himself hesitating.

'But . . . I wouldn't know where to start,' he protested. 'I'm not even sure we'd be allowed . . .'

Suddenly a third voice burst unexpectedly into their conversation.

'We'll do it!' said Polly.

Dollar Island

Sherman H. Kruud, owner of the mighty Kruud Kola Corporation, peered through the cockpit window at the palm-fringed dollar sign nestling in the silver-blue ocean below him. 'I sure do love watching money grow,' he reflected smugly, as his private jet continued its descent and Dollar Island – *his* Dollar Island – rose up to meet him. He prepared to land, stretching an extra long safety belt around his waist before screeching on to the heat-shimmered runway, which cut through the centre of the dusty, S-shaped island like a giant down-stroke. Kruud brought the plane to rest at the top end of the island, nose to nose with its own reflection in the sea of cool, tranquil glass which stretched across the front of his gleaming white villa. The vast window had been installed so that Kruud could admire the plane – and with it his success – from the comfort of his lounge. It was interrupted only by the entrance to the house where, standing between two white marble columns, Kruud's stooped, grey-haired butler prepared to welcome his employer home from his latest business trip. The elderly manservant straightened his tie nervously, the stiff white collar so wide around his withered neck that his head looked as though it might sink into it, like a frightened tortoise retreating into its shell.

The outside world held no such fears for Kruud. He stepped down from the plane – wearing a white suit that looked two sizes too small for him, and a matching cowboy hat that looked two sizes too big – knowing, as he had always known, that the world and everything in it, including the butler, existed solely for his benefit.

The manservant stepped forward, his thin, down-turned mouth stretched wide across a pale and hollow face that looked as though every smile had been sucked out of it.

'Welcome back, Mr Kruud.'

'Have you got ma milk and meringues ready?' Kruud demanded.

'Yes, Mr Kruud. They're waiting for you by the pool.'

'Are they extra white? Y'know I like ma meringues as white as angel poo.'

'Yes, Mr Kruud, they're . . .' The butler hesitated. '. . . just how you like them.'

'Good,' replied Kruud, 'an' that reminds me, I ran over a couple of juicy pigeons on the runway. If you get to them before the alligators you can have pigeon pie for supper.'

'Thank you, Mr Kruud,' the butler replied, meekly. 'I'm very grateful.'

'You sure as hell should be,' said Kruud, marching past him into the house. 'I had to swerve re-e-eal hard to hit 'em.'

He strode through the house to the huge sun-soaked terrace which lay on the other side. Into it were set two pools – one a large swimming pool in the shape of a dollar sign, like the island itself, the other a small circular pool decorated like a circus ring, with a red, white and blue star painted on the bottom and a metal hoop suspended above the water near the centre. Beside it, supported a metre or so from the ground on a specially made stand, a dazzling silver tray lay waiting with Kruud's milk and a perfectly stacked pyramid of miniature white meringues.

'Let's have some dollar-kissin' service round here, Arthur,' Kruud called into the water. At the sound of his voice, a dark shape emerged from the bottom of the pool and stuck its nose haughtily above the surface. Then, recognising Kruud, the nose's whiskery owner disappeared again, circling the hoop in a blur just below the surface before jumping through it with a sideways roll and landing back in the water close to the pool steps.

'Quit showin' off, boy,' said Kruud. 'Ma meringues are turnin' gooey.'

'Arf!' barked the seal and clambered, glistening, out of the pool. It shuffled over to the tray, confidently lifting it off the stand with its nose and carrying it over to Kruud.

'Arf!' it said.

Kruud took the glass of milk and a huge handful of meringues, and the seal returned the tray to its stand.

'You think that's a clever trick, Arthur?' Kruud asked the seal, flicking a meringue into his mouth.

'Arf!' replied the seal, diving back into the water.

'Well, it ain't nothin' compared to this,' said Kruud, stepping over to the low wall on the edge of the terrace which looked out over Dollar Island.

His house was built on top of a cliff facing south, so he could see the whole island stretched out in front of him. The view was dominated by a volcano, which squatted, immense and immovable like a giant limpet, on the opposite end of the island. From its mouth an unbroken trail of poisonous black smoke could be seen rising thousands of feet into the air, before being caught by the breeze bound for the mainland. The volcano was extinct, of course. Over the years Kruud had bought dozens of them around the world and located his Kruud Kola bottling factories deep inside the caves and chasms beneath them. He had discovered that volcanic islands were not only cheap to buy, but far from the prying eyes of all those finger-wagging do-gooders and environmentalists. For years they had buzzed around him like flies around a cowpat, accusing him of polluting the planet and helping to kill off the lesser spotted this, or the long-nosed, short-tailed, hump-backed that. Well, he didn't have to swish them away any longer. His islands were miles from anywhere, and from their hidden factories he could dump as much filth into the air as he liked, safe in the knowledge that any passing ship or aeroplane would simply mistake it for the natural outpourings of a grumpy old volcano.

'Now *that*'s what I call a trick, Arthur,' he said, flicking another meringue into his mouth.

He checked his diamond-studded watch, then turned back to the house.

'Clubs!' he called out.

Moments later the butler staggered out to him, his creaky old knees buckling under the weight of the white leather golf bag rattling over his shoulder. Kruud whipped a club out of the bag as the butler dropped a golf ball into his hand. Kruud inspected the ball, wiping a speck of dirt from it on to the butler's forehead, before firing it off the edge of the cliff towards the volcano. It soared out over Dollar Island, landing close to one of the alligators which inhabited the swampland either side of the runway. Kruud stamped his foot.

'Dammit, missed.'

He gulped down a mouthful of milk, then took another ball from the butler, determined to give at least one of the alligators a lump on its head before his visitor arrived.

Unlike alligators, visitors to the island were quite rare.

Normally it was off limits to all but his most trusted business associates, but this was different. This visitor claimed to have an offer that would make him, once and for all, the richest man in the world. What's more, she seemed to know everything about him. She knew about the child workers that toiled like slaves in his worldwide network of factories, lured away from their dirt-poor families with false promises of proper jobs, fair wages and decent food in their stomachs. She knew about the bamboo-masters, bullies he employed to keep his young, half-starved workforce in its place with regular stinging swipes from their bamboo canes. Most worryingly, she knew his biggest secret of all: that the mystery ingredient which gave every bottle of Kruud Kola its distinctive taste – making it irresistible to millions of children around the world – was nothing more than a spoonful of the same sticky black toxic waste that he burned in his factories to power the bottling machines. Waste with taste, he liked to call it.

He launched another ball into orbit. Missed again. Something was bothering him.

'How in the dollar-kissin' world does she know so much about me, Arthur?'

The seal rolled over in the water, turning on to its back.

'Arf!' it replied.

'No, I ain't got a clue either, boy. But I sure as hell am gonna find out.'

A horn sounded. Kruud grabbed the rim of his hat and peered over the wall to the wooden jetty at the foot of the cliff. Moolah and Luka, his two most feared bamboo-masters, were busy tying his private yacht *Sherman* alongside it, having that minute returned from the mainland with Kruud's mysterious visitor. The jetty was reached via several hundred steps which had been cut into the cliff face. Kruud never used the steps himself – his personal lift inside the house took him down to the jetty in a matter of seconds. But watching everyone else struggle up and down them was one of his greatest pleasures, especially when they were bent double under the weight of sea-going provisions and equipment. Winners took the lift, losers took the stairs – that was the way of the world according to Kruud, and he never tired of reminding himself and everyone else about which group he belonged to. So, pausing only to toss Arthur a fishy reward from a nearby bucket, he walked back inside the house and stepped into the lift.

The two bamboo-masters were waiting for him at the bottom, their canes tucked like pirate cutlasses into their belts, alongside the set of keys that each carried to operate the factory machines. Like most bamboo-masters they had begun by working in the factory, but had flourished under its brutal regime, growing fit and strong on a mixture of hard work and the extra food which they forced the smaller, weaker children to hand over to them. Kruud was quick to spot talent and use it to his advantage, so once they were old enough, the toughest and meanest of his workers were allowed to become bamboo-masters. In return for keeping the factory running ruthlessly round the clock, they were given a comfortable black uniform with matching flip-flops, their own corrugated-iron hut to sleep in and decent food. They even received modest wages, which they were free to spend whenever they picked up supplies from the mainland. Such visits gave them plenty of opportunities to escape Kruud's employment, but they rarely took them. Instead, the bamboo-masters were fiercely loyal to their boss, enjoying more respect and power on Dollar Island than they were ever likely to find elsewhere, which made it a position to which many aspired. Even so, few candidates dared attempt the challenge – known as 'walking the runway' – which each had to complete successfully in order to prove themselves worthy. For most, setting out on foot along the runway meant certain death, a punishment even worse than 'walking the plank'. Because, whilst the alligators which lived in the swamps either side never troubled Kruud's plane, or the armour-plated golf buggies he used to travel between the fenced-off safety of his villa and the factory, they were quick to sniff easier prey. So, 'walking the runway' was usually reserved for the worst factory trouble-makers or the occasional uninvited volcanologist. For aspiring bamboo-masters, though, it was the ultimate test of their speed and courage. Only the fittest could hope to survive the attentions of the alligators. Fewer still could cut their own bamboo cane from around one of the swamps on the way to become a fully fledged bamboo-master. Moolah had passed the test several years earlier, daring even to snatch one of Kruud's golf balls from the gaping jaws of an alligator on the way. This she kept in her pocket for good luck, and to remind herself that she could outdo any boy. The only girl in a family of thirteen, her parents had sold her to Kruud as soon as she was old enough to stick a label on a Kola bottle, believing that of all their children she, rather than any of her ten brothers, would be least able to survive the wretched poverty in which they lived. Since that tearful, bewildering day, she had devoted herself to proving them wrong, becoming twice as strong, twice as fast and twice as mean as any of the other bamboo-masters, all of whom were boys. In so doing she had become as unpopular with them as she was with the children in the factory. But she didn't care. At least Mr Kruud, she hoped, could see just how wrong her mother and father had been.

Luka tapped her coldly on the shoulder. Kruud had arrived.

'Where is she?' he asked them. Their unsmiling crew-cut heads nodded towards the end of the jetty, where a human matchstick stood motionless with her back to them, quietly watching the trail of smoke rising from the mouth of the volcano.

Kruud was encouraged by what he saw. His spindly visitor certainly looked dressed for business in her pink two-piece suit and matching stiletto shoes. The expensive snake-skin briefcase held in a claw-like grip at her side seemed to confirm that she was there to talk about money, rather than to wag a bony finger at him for feeding his workers on squashed runway pigeons and Arthur's leftovers. So far so good. Kruud bounced across the springy wooden planks to introduce himself.

'If your business offer is half as big as that volcano, ma'am,' he joked, stepping alongside her to share the view, 'then Sherman H. Kruud is mighty pleased to meet you.'

The woman smiled. 'Oh, it's much bigger than that,' she replied confidently, 'but half is precisely what it will cost you.'

Kruud cocked his head to one side, puzzled.

'Half of what, ma'am?' he asked.

Venetia Pike cast her eyes around the island, before turning back to face him.

'Half of everything, ssssweetie,' she replied.

Power-sharing

Polly wasn't the only person to have secretly listened in on Tom's conversation with Hopper Hawkins.

Venetia Pike had heard every word. Kruud's spindle-boned visitor had been trapped under Shipley Manor ever since the Fizzle wrenched it out of the ground and carried it down to the sea. As the water had swirled around the house, Polly's favourite tree sculpture – the octopus which Slugbucket had fashioned from the roots of a giant oak tree – had appeared to come to life and attack her. Furiously she had fought it off, unaware that it was trying to protect her. When she sank, exhausted, below the surface of the moat, it had pressed her up against the building's uprooted foundations, cupping its tentacles around her like a hand shielding a fragile flame from the wind. Whilst a bubble of Fizzle gas formed around her head the octopus had pinned her there, deflecting the deadly barrage of swirling rocks and debris that battered the underside of the house on its roller-coaster ride down the valley. Once Shipley Manor reached the sea and the Fizzle's fury subsided, the tentacles returned to their natural, wooden form, trapping her inside like the bars of an underwater prison cell. Despite frantic efforts to escape her watery jail, Pike remained there for the whole month that Shipley Manor spent in dock, breathing the Fizzle gas and devouring any fish foolish enough to stray too close to her desperate, lightning-quick grasp.

Of course she needed water to survive, too. So, like Hopper Hawkins all those years before, she had pressed her wrinkled lips up against the outside of the bubble and sucked in mouthfuls of Fizzle. She had tasted the Fizzle before at Shipley Manor, but to no effect. This time she 'Got the Fizzle' immediately, suddenly feeling part of everything and everyone in the world around her.

She hated it.

Unlike everyone else who experienced it, the feeling of being part of one big family made her feel sick. What she hated most was the idea that everything in nature was her equal. What utter nonsense. She was Queen of the Castle and always had been, and she wasn't about to join this or any other family, unless it was to become head of it. It didn't matter how much of the Fizzle she drank. Since there wasn't a single spark of goodness in her, it simply couldn't ignite the flame of friendship that warmed everyone else who drank it. So Pike's mind remained a booby trap, her heart a cold, barren desert without so much as a tumbleweed of kindness rolling through it. Most chillingly of all, as her body remained trapped under Shipley Manor, it continued to breathe in more and more and more of the most powerful gas in the universe.

She had begun hearing Polly and Tom's voices almost straightaway. Soft and muffled at first, within a few days their conversations had become as clear as though they were standing next to her. It didn't take long for Pike to realise that the Fizzle gas had created an invisible connection between them. She had discovered its power, and until she thought of a way to escape the octopus's rigid grip, she had nothing to do except learn how to use it.

And learn she did. Over time she discovered that she could read the minds of not just Polly and Tom, but anyone who had recently drunk the Fizzle. For several minutes after they'd drunk it she would catch glimpses of what they were thinking. This power far exceeded Polly and Tom's. Whilst they could tell what people around them were feeling, she alone could hear the Captain pondering over various travel destinations, or see the numbers spinning around inside Seymour's head as he made mental calculations. She imagined the huge advantages she could gain by serving Fizzle to business rivals during negotiations, or the fortunes she could win from multimillionaires unlucky enough to play poker with her, unaware that she could tell which cards they were holding. Reading their Fizzle-refreshed minds would be quite some party trick. But her winnings at cards would be nothing but pocket money. With such power at her disposal she knew she should be able to achieve almost unimaginable wealth.

And, as soon as Hopper made himself known to Tom and asked him to complete his mission, she had known how. But she would need help. That night she spent hours searching her own memory for inspiration, but it was Hopper who provided her with the answer. She had been listening to him talking to his great granddaughter Scarlett. Although Pike's connection was with Hopper, after a month breathing in the gas her powers had grown so far ahead of Polly and Tom's that she could hear what Scarlett was saying to him too, just as clearly as if she were hearing it through her own ears. Scarlett was telling him about a man, a very rich man, a man of dubious business practices and low cunning who, much to the disgust of Scarlett and her environmentalist friends, had for years continued to pollute the planet and poison children's stomachs in pursuit of his own wealth. Ruthless and despicable, Scarlett had called him, and seemingly above the law despite the vast dossier of evidence she had compiled against him. This she had proceeded to recount in great detail to Hopper. And the more Pike heard about how cruel and greedy and powerful Sherman H. Kruud was, the more impressed she had become. When eventually she heard that he kept reptiles on his island – albeit of a more toothsome variety than the snakes she so admired – well, that was it. She knew he was the man for her. There had been much to do that night. She would need to escape from underneath Shipley Manor before it sailed, and take a crate of Fizzle away with her. The first part was easy. From inside her blouse she removed the large fish bone which she'd spent weeks sharpening against Shipley Manor's foundations. Then, as she sawed her way to freedom, she had sneaked into Polly's mind for the first time. The next morning, just before sunrise, Venetia Pike had pulled herself out of the water like a poisonous splinter and, as the wound sealed behind her, collected the crate of Fizzle which had so conveniently been left out on the drawbridge.

And now, three days later, here she was face to face with Kruud in his lift, about to make him an offer he couldn't refuse.

Up close, the first thing Kruud noticed about Pike was the smell. She had eaten nothing but raw fish during her month under Shipley Manor, and their discarded carcasses had accumulated, rotting slowly so that the water surrounding her had come to resemble stale fish soup. She had marinated in the rancid remains for so long that it had soaked deep into her skin, and despite hours of painful scrubbing, her smart, freshly laundered business suit, her new white-blonde wig and her perfectly painted fingernails simply couldn't disguise the fact that she smelled like a bucket of old fish-guts. And neither, after endless prodding and poking, had she dislodged the two decaying fish bones which remained wedged stubbornly in her back teeth. Kruud fumbled for his handkerchief, pretending to blow his nose in order to avoid her haddocky breath. She looked as though she'd been in the water for as long as a fish, too. Her whole body was covered in the same kind of wrinkles that appear on fingertips after a long bath. Except that these hadn't faded away once she was dry. They had stayed, a lasting souvenir of her month underwater. Kruud took a deep breath before tucking the handkerchief back into his pocket.

'You seem to know an awful lot about me, ma'am,' he said, puffing out his chest. 'I hope for your sake you haven't come here to threaten me.'

Pike smiled reassuringly.

'Relax, Sherman. Although I'm sure the world would be fasssscinated to know what you put in Kruud Kola, I have no desire to tell them. On the contrary, I rather admire your methods. That's why I think we'll make such a winning team. In any case, what I've come to offer you is so sssstupendous that I won't need to resort to anything quite so . . .' She sighed in mock regret. '. . . delicious as blackmail.'

The lift opened and they stepped out into Kruud's lounge. Arthur shuffled over to them, sniffing the air hopefully before retreating, disappointed, when he discovered that Pike wasn't a real fish after all.

'I call this the White Room,' Kruud explained.

His visitor looked around. True to its name, everything in the room was white. White paintings hung on white walls, white lights shone down from the white ceiling, and white marble statues stood around like all-white chess pieces on an all-white chessboard. Kruud flushed with pride as he led Pike towards the vast window on the far side of the room, behind which stood his plane, elegant and angular against the dazzling blue Caribbean sky. In front of the window two bulging white sofas faced each other like a pair of sumo wrestlers, separated by a frosted glass coffee table upon which the butler had just finished laying more milk and meringues for Kruud, and tea and biscuits for his guest. Kruud waved his employee away contemptuously and flopped back on to one of the sofas. Pike sat down opposite him – a vivid pink gash against the white leather. She turned to admire the jet peering down at them, its nose pressed close to the glass as though it were eavesdropping.

'What a ssssimply ssssplendid jet,' she complimented him. 'I see you appreciate the trappings of wealth, Sherman – the private jets, the luxury yachts, the solid gold toenail clippers. And rightly so. As one of the richest people in the world you deserve the best of everything.'

Kruud sprawled back in his seat, luxuriating in Pike's words like a fat cat having its tummy tickled.

'You better believe it, ma'am. And for your information my toenail clippers are studded with diamonds.'

'Even more impressive,' Pike continued, leaning forward in her seat as though to pass on bad news, 'but not quite as impressive as Mr Robovich's new jumbo jet.'

Kruud sat up. Robovich was one of his super-rich rivals.

'He's bought his own jumbo jet?'

'I'm told it even has its own sssswimming pool,' Pike informed him, smiling. 'Indoors, of course.'

Kruud looked through the window at his own aeroplane. Suddenly it seemed a lot smaller.

'Damn show-off!'

'And I presume you've heard about Mr Ching's new yacht,' Pike continued. Kruud shook his head.

'Not only is it twice as long as yours, Sherman, but rumour has it that the bottom half detaches and converts into a luxury submarine.'

Kruud flicked another meringue. It missed his mouth and skidded across the marble floor behind him.

'What's your point, ma'am?'

Pike leaned closer.

'Wouldn't you like to own the biggest plane in the world, Sherman – the longest yacht, the tallest skyscraper, the fattest diamond? Wouldn't you like to make Mr Robovich, and Mr Ching, and Mr Punjabootee and all your other super-rich rivals look as though they don't have two gold taps to rub together?'

'That's exactly what I reckon on doing, ma'am.'

'So where are you now on the list of the world's richest people?' she challenged him.

'Seventh,' he replied, 'and mighty proud of it, too.'

'*Seventh!*' repeated Pike scornfully. 'If making money was an Olympic sport you wouldn't even get a bronze medal for coming seventh. We both know that winning is all about coming *first*, Sherman, about being number *one*, about standing on *top* of the winners' rostrum with no one above you.'

'An' I'm gonna get there, ma'am, make no mistake.'

'Yes, but when, Sherman? Within the next five years? Or ten? Or twenty? How can you be sure that when you finally hit the top spot you're not too old to enjoy it?'

Kruud looked thoughtful. 'Good question, ma'am, and I suppose you're going to tell me you have the answer.'

Pike nodded. 'That's right. You ssssee, Sherman, I can guarantee to make you the richest man in the world within . . .' She held up a wizened forefinger. '. . . one month.'

Now it was Kruud's turn to lean forward.

'How?' he asked.

Pike pulled a bottle of Fizzle from her briefcase and placed it on the table.

'With this.'

Kruud slumped back in his sofa. Another fizzy drink. If he had a dollar for every time some loser tried to sell him a new fizzy drink recipe, he would already be the richest man in the world.

'Kruud Kola is by far the most popular fizzy drink on the planet,' he explained, wearily. 'Why the hell would I be interested in another one?'

'Because of what it *does*, Sherman.'

'An' what's that, ma'am?' asked Kruud, glancing at his watch.

'It makes almost everyone who drinks it . . .' Her mouth turned down at the corners, as though she were trying to swallow a mouthful of fish-guts. '. . . get on.'

'Get on what?' Kruud replied, impatiently. 'Get on a bus? Get on my nerves? What?'

Pike shook her head, smiling.

'Just . . . get on.'

Kruud raised his eyebrows. Suddenly Pike had regained his attention.

'You mean . . . it makes them *like* each other?'

'Preccccisely,' she confirmed. 'As though they're all members of one big happy family. Hideous, isn't it?'

'You said "almost everyone".'

'That's right,' Pike explained. 'Whoever drinks it must believe that anything is possible. Small children do that quite naturally of course – ask any tooth fairy. But even when they've grown up, plenty of them still manage to believe that tomorrow's weather forecast might be right, or that flying saucers could really exist.'

Kruud smiled and plucked a crisp new fifty-dollar note from the rim of his hat.

'Personally, I prefer to put my faith in something a little more down to earth,' he explained, before pressing the banknote to his face and slowly breathing in its aroma as though it were a beautiful scented rose.

'Aaah, the heavenly cent . . . You know I have to put this fizzy drink of yours to the test, don't you, ma'am?'

'Of course,' she replied, 'but make sure you don't drink any yourself. I don't want to risk my new business partner turning into a big ssssoftie.'

Kruud tucked the banknote back into his hat and picked up a phone from the coffee table.

'Moolah, are those two miniature tearaways on the night shift still tryin' to kill each other? Good. Bring 'em here, right now.'

Pike continued:

'Can you imagine what a disaster it would be if everyone went around liking each other? Just think what would happen if *you* drank it, Sherman. Suddenly you'd find yourself wanting to give your workers proper food and wages, you'd start putting health warnings on the side of every Kruud Kola bottle or removing your famous "mystery ingredient" altogether. Your costs would soar, your sales would plummet. Before you knew it you'd have to sell your jet. But who would buy it? Certainly not Mr Ching. His company makes fighter planes and warships. Without wars being fought all over the world Mr Ching's bank balance would sink faster than his private submarine. Don't you see? This fizzy water has more power to change the world than every atomic weapon in it. And that power could soon be under our control, Sherman. Just imagine what the richest and most powerful people in the world will pay us *not* to use it.'

'Us?'

'Ussss, Sherman. Only I can bring the Fizzle to you, and only the Kruud Kola Corporation can threaten to bottle it up and distribute it worldwide. Together we can demand half of Ching Industries and countless other businesses like it, in return for ssssealing the Fizzle into this volcano of yours so that no one ever drinks it. We won't just be rich, Sherman. We won't even be super-rich. We'll end up owning half the planet.'

Kruud looked down at the bottle.

'Who else knows about this?' he asked.

'Oh, word's getting round that there's something special about the water,' Pike replied. 'Only a few weeks ago it ripped an entire house out of the ground and carried it down to the sea – not the sort of thing you can keep quiet. A few people have drunk it too, but only four in the world, including me, have – shall we say – "absorbed" some of its rather sssspecial powers.'

'An' what are those, ma'am?'

'One of them,' she said, fixing him with a stare from beneath her long false eyelashes, 'is the ability to read minds.'

Kruud shifted awkwardly in his seat. Only moments before he'd been thinking about feeding his visitor to the alligators.

'Don't worry,' she continued, smiling at his discomfort, 'you haven't drunk any Fizzle from that bottle. But if you had, for the next few minutes your mind would be as easy for me to read as an open book. Imagine having me at your side, Sherman, able to tell you what your enemies and business rivals are thinking. We'd be unbeatable.'

'An' the other three?'

'Pah! Two children and a bedridden old man, and none of them breathed the gas for more than a few seconds. Don't worry, Sherman, their abilities are puny compared to mine. I can take care of them.'

Just then Moolah appeared in the doorway. She was holding two ragged, barefoot boys apart at arm's length, whilst they lashed out at each other like a pair of fighting dogs.

'Pepe Gonzalo and Paco Martinez,' she told her boss.

'Their families have been feudin' over the same scrap of farmland for generations,' Kruud explained to his guest. 'First their grandfathers killed each other fighting for it, then their fathers did the same. Sure as hell if we didn't keep these two hotheads in different work gangs they'd kill each other, too.'

Kruud watched the two boys spitting insults and accusations at each other in their native language, oblivious to everything else around them. So much hate – the perfect test for this new fizzy drink.

'Speak civilised!' he barked, finally. 'You know the rule: learn to speak English or Alligator, one or the other.'

For a moment they stopped, before launching themselves at each other again, their fear of Kruud exceeded only by their hatred of each other. Only Moolah's long arms and vice-like grip kept their flailing fists and feet from finding their targets. Shaking his head at their behaviour, Kruud picked up the bottle and swaggered over to one of the boys. He gripped his chin, pulling his face sharply towards the bottle held out in front of him.

'Drink this, boy,' he commanded.

The boy obeyed, feeling the bamboo-master's grip on his arm tighten to remind him of what would happen if he refused. Kruud retrieved the bottle and turned to the other boy.

'Now you.'

He retrieved the bottle again and stepped back, as though he had just lit a large firework.

'Let them go, Moolah.'

'But, Mr Kruud, if they injure each other we'll be short-handed in the factory tonight.'

'It doesn't matter, just do as I say.'

Moolah nodded and released her grip.

The boys appeared not to notice. They stared ahead for a full minute, dazed and motionless, as though suddenly they'd woken up in a strange place, with no idea where to go, or what to do next. Then, before Moolah could stop them, they flung themselves at each other. But instead of fighting they clung to each other. Kruud watched in open-mouthed horror as, with tears rolling down their cheeks, the anger of the two boys dissolved into regret, and their mutual hatred turned to friendship. There was no doubt: the Fizzle had proved itself.

Kruud turned away, his face contorted with disgust.

'Gee, that's revolting – I think I'm gonna be sick. Get them out of my sight, Moolah.'

He handed Moolah the half-empty bottle.

'And whilst you're at it, pour the rest of this poison down the nearest sink.'

As soon as they were alone Kruud turned to Pike and held out his hand.

'You got yourself a deal, ma'am,' he said.

A Hidden Message

Jamaica. The word had been buzzing around inside Polly's head like a fly searching for an open window. It was somewhere she had always wanted to go, but no more so than a dozen other places the Captain had told her about. So why couldn't she stop thinking about it? It was as though there was someone inside her head telling her to go there. But the voice didn't belong to Tom, or Hopper. It was more of a low whisper, albeit one that grew quickly into such a deafening cacophony that all other thoughts were extinguished. Jamaica. The same thing had happened the night before they left the docks, words flying around inside her head, telling her to leave a crate of Fizzle on the drawbridge before going to bed. She had no idea why she had done it, only that by doing so the words would go away. That was more than three days ago now. Since then the Captain had sailed Shipley Manor back and forth along the English coast, testing out the new paddle-wheels and mastering the controls of the world's first floating country house. He had also wanted to find out whether the Fizzle would remain with them or decide to go its own way. So far it had stayed, allowing the Captain to steer Shipley Manor along its own course but moving with it so that the house remained in its centre. Now, with its sea trials completed, Shipley Manor was at last ready to set off on its maiden voyage. All that remained was to decide where to go – something which the Captain was finding difficult. Because although he had done everything possible to make Shipley Manor seaworthy, he knew that the old stone walls simply weren't built to survive the mountainous seas that might be encountered on a long voyage. Much as he enjoyed pitting his wits against the elements, he knew that he should be cautious.

Polly had no such reservations. She and the rest of the crew were at the kitchen table, tucking into one of the Captain's fruit cakes whilst studying the world map spread out like a tablecloth in front of them.

'It has to be Jamaica, I just know it,' she kept

saying, even though she couldn't say why.

The Captain shook his head. 'The Caribbean is too far, Polly. Much as I'd like to visit Mamma Mango's Beach Café again, the journey would take us at least ten days, even with the Fizzle speeding us along. And if it leaves us halfway across the Atlantic and a storm brews up we could be in big trouble. Don't forget, the Caribbean is a hurricane zone. I can't risk Shipley Manor being caught up in one of those, especially with you and Tom and Calypso on board.'

Maggie nodded her agreement. Calypso wriggled around in her arms and nodded too.

'Calypso's nod doesn't count,' Polly said firmly. 'She's just copying.'

The Captain turned to Tom. 'What do you think, shipmate?'

Polly's eyes narrowed as she watched him answer.

'Well, actually . . .' he said, sucking air between his teeth, '. . . I think you're right – it makes sense to test Shipley Manor out on a short voyage first. Sorry, Polly.'

Polly huffed and folded her arms.

'Why do you always have to be so sensible, Tom?'

Slugbucket thought he had the solution.

'P'raps we should just 'op around then,' he suggested, 'loik them pesky rabbits what used to 'op around me vegetable patch. First we could 'op over to France, then we could 'op down the coast to Portugal, an' from there we could 'op along to Spain. We could even 'op over to that little island there,' he added, pointing to the map.

Polly flicked it away with her finger. 'That's a currant, Slugbucket.'

The Captain smiled. 'Even so, I think Slugbucket might have the answer,' he said. 'We could stay within sight of land the whole time, and from Spain we could even make the short hop over to Africa. I could take you to a Moroccan bazaar, Polly. I'm sure we'd find some wonderful fabrics for your costumes.'

But Polly was adamant.

'We have to go to Jamaica,' she said, clenching her fists. 'I don't know why, but we have to. Why won't any of you trust me?'

The Captain shook his head. 'I'm sorry, Polly, but unless you can come up with a good reason to risk such a long journey my decision is made. Tomorrow morning we set sail for France.'

Polly remained slumped in her seat, pushing a cake crumb around South America with her fingernail whilst everyone except Tom and Seymour left the kitchen. For once Seymour hadn't said a word during the meeting. Instead, his eyes had been fixed on Polly and Tom, studying them with a mixture of puzzlement and suspicion.

'I've been carrying out more experiments with the Fizzle,' he said eventually. 'Would you meet me in the Crow's Nest in half an hour? I'd like to show you the results.'

Tom nodded. 'Just us?'

'Just you,' Seymour confirmed, wheeling himself out of the room.

That's odd, thought Tom. Then he remembered something even odder.

'Why do you want to go to Jamaica so much, Polly?' he asked.

'I don't know,' she replied. 'It's as though there's a voice telling me to. That's not all. When I close my eyes I can see the word "Jamaica" painted in bright pink letters behind my eyelids. Perhaps it's something to do with Hopper's mission.'

'It's our mission now,' Tom reminded her. 'We accepted it, didn't we? Even so I don't see what going to the Caribbean could have to do with sharing the Fizzle.'

Half an hour later they arrived in the Crow's Nest, or as Seymour sometimes called it, the Fizzics laboratory.

Because for the past month he had done nothing there but experiment on the Fizzle. Spurred on by the spectacular success of his Fizzleworks display, and inspired by the awesome power that the water had demonstrated when plucking Shipley Manor out of the ground, he had become obsessed with finding out everything he could about it. The circular room was lined with empty Fizzle crates, their contents transferred into an array of glass containers – shallow dishes, jam jars, mixing bowls, medicine bottles, fish tanks and test tubes – which covered the worktop. Some of these were connected through a network of tubes to pieces of equipment that Seymour had scavenged from the kitchen – kettles, food mixers, liquidisers, Edna's old steam iron – to create elaborate pieces of apparatus with which to spin, boil, filter or freeze the Fizzle. He had gathered together numerous other substances too – washing-up liquid, glue, rubber solution, different kinds of oils, cleaning fluids, polishes and paints – all of which he had mixed with the Fizzle to create new formulas. These concoctions now lined the shelves in the original Fizzle bottles, each clearly labelled with a description of the formula it contained and the effect, if any, that it had. And sitting amidst this sprawling Fizzle refinery was something which Polly and Tom had never expected to see again: Slugbucket's orange bucket – full to the brim with fat, slimy slugs.

'Slugbucket left it on the steps of his caravan,' Seymour explained. 'Somehow it survived the journey down the valley along with all the slugs inside. They've been helping me with my experiments.'

'Don't you want to show everyone else what you've been doing too, Seymour?' Polly asked him.

'Not yet,' he explained. 'There's something I want to show you and Tom first.'

He swivelled round in his chair and picked up a coffee-maker. Tom had seen his father use one just like it at home. It consisted of a tall glass jug, inside which a plunger on the end of a metal rod could be raised or lowered through a hole in the lid. Every morning at breakfast Tom's father would tip a spoonful of coffee granules into the jug, then fill it with hot water and replace the lid. Once the coffee had brewed he would press the plunger down inside the jar, pushing the granules to the bottom whilst the hot, smooth coffee filtered up through fine holes in the plunger to the space above.

'I call it a Fizzle Filter,' Seymour explained. 'As you can see, it's like a normal coffee-maker, except that I've made the holes in the plunger so fine that liquid can no longer pass through it. But gas can. So, when I fill the jug with Fizzle and press the plunger down, the gas contained in all those tiny bubbles is squeezed through into the space above. Let me show you.'

Seymour filled the jug almost to the top with Fizzle, then inserted the plunger, pushing it down until it rested on top of the liquid. Next, to Polly and Tom's surprise, he plucked two slugs from the orange bucket and placed them on top of the plunger. Finally he put on the airtight lid, sealing them in. He handed Polly and Tom a pair of goggles and put a pair on himself.

'The first time I did this, Nautipus nearly jumped out of his fur,' he explained, pulling on a pair of thick gardening gloves. 'I pressed too hard and the jug exploded. I discovered that when the Fizzle is put under too much pressure the bubbles start to pop in two. The trouble is that once they've started they can't stop. An instant after they divide they expand to their original size again, which increases the pressure still further, which makes them divide again, and expand again, so that within a split second each bubble has turned into several million, all crammed into the same confined space. You can imagine what happened to that poor jug. I'm still finding bits of it now.'

He pulled down his goggles.

'Luckily I'm so used to my experiments blowing up that I was wearing these at the time. Now, stand well back.'

Once Polly and Tom had moved to the other side of the room, Seymour crossed both hands on top of the plunger and began, slowly and firmly, to press down. Tom watched the Fizzle carefully, and although the plunger seemed barely to move he could see thousands of tiny gas bubbles rising towards it, before being pushed through into the space above. When all the bubbles had been forced out of the Fizzle, Seymour took his hands off the plunger.

'There,' he said, removing his goggles.

'Is that it?' asked Polly, slightly disappointed.

'No, that's just the beginning of the experiment,' Seymour replied. 'The slugs are now breathing the Fizzle gas that was forced through the plunger. It's only a thimbleful, I know, but it's enough to fill their tiny lungs. Now watch carefully.'

He waited a few more seconds, then lifted the lid and removed the slugs. The first he dropped into a matchbox which he slipped into his trouser pocket. The second he placed on the desktop in front of three upturned egg cups.

'There's a tasty little snack hidden under one of them,' he explained, 'a piece of lettuce from Slugbucket's new roof garden. As you can see, the slug has no idea it's there.'

Sure enough the slug made no attempt to move towards any of the egg cups. But then Seymour lifted up the middle egg cup, revealing the scrap of lettuce underneath. Immediately the slug slithered over to it and began nibbling the leaf.

'Now this is the interesting bit,' said Seymour. He picked up the slug and pushed it into another matchbox which he asked Tom to hide in his pocket. Then he retrieved the first slug and placed it in front of the same three egg cups. Straightaway it headed for the middle one containing the lettuce.

'You see, it *knows*,' Seymour explained. 'The other slug has told it where lunch is, even though they've been separated from each other the whole time. Don't you see? Breathing the Fizzle gas has given them the ability to communicate with each other even when they're apart. It has connected their minds.'

Seymour sat back in his chair, gently tapping the armrests with his fingers.

'Now, you two,' he grinned, 'is there anything you'd like to tell me?'

Polly and Tom looked down at their feet for a few moments. Then Tom turned back to Seymour.

'You're right,' he admitted, retrieving the matchbox from his pocket and putting it on the worktop. 'Polly and I can talk to each other like that, too. We've been able to do it since we breathed in the Fizzle gas last month.'

Seymour slapped his armrests in triumph. 'I knew it!'

'We were going to tell you all,' Polly explained, suddenly aware of a new fondness for lettuce. 'We were really, except we wanted to find out what we could do first.'

Seymour nodded.

'I don't blame you for keeping it to yourself for a while,' he replied. 'It's always best to find out as much as you can about something before announcing it from the rooftops. That's why I haven't shown anyone else what I'm about to show you.'

'You mean there's more?' asked Polly.

'Oh yes,' Seymour replied, 'and it's quite a discovery, I can tell you.'

He picked up a wire coat hanger from the desk and formed it into a hoop. Then he dipped it into a bucket of Fizzle on the floor.

'It's my new formula: a hundred parts Fizzle, ten parts washing-up liquid, two parts rubber solution and a drop of something with a name so long that it would take me all day to spell it.'

He took a deep breath and blew through the hoop. A bubble emerged on the other side, growing to the size of a football before detaching itself and hovering above Polly and Tom's heads.

Polly and Tom watched. They'd seen this before.

'Now watch,' said Seymour. He dipped the hoop back into the bucket, recoating it in the new Fizzle formula. This time he held it out in front of him like a frying pan. Then he took another slug from the bucket and dropped it into the hoop. As it hit the transparent skin the slug neither broke the skin nor rebounded. Instead, the skin stretched as the slug passed through, finally springing away from the coat hanger and forming a perfect bubble around the slug. There the bubble stayed, hovering above the floor like a transparent flying machine, its sluggy pilot unharmed in the centre. Next, Seymour took the scrap of lettuce from under the egg cup and held it in front of the bubble. Immediately the hungry slug's little antennae stretched out for it, moving the bubble towards it. Then Seymour moved the lettuce from side to side. Each time the slug's antennae stretched towards it, the bubble responded and changed course.

'You see,' Seymour explained, excitedly, 'the slug is steering it.'

He looked up at them, grinning from ear to ear. 'I call it Fizzle Flying Formula, 3F for short. It works with heavier things, too. I dropped a big juicy grapefruit through there yesterday, expecting it to break through the Fizzle skin and splatter on the ground. But it floated. There's no gravity inside, you see,' he told them, 'and the bubble's spinning so fast it doesn't have time to fall.'

The experiment over, Seymour touched the bubble with his fingertip and it popped. 'That's the biggest problem with it,' he said, catching the falling slug in his hand and placing it back in its matchbox. 'The slightest touch and the bubble bursts. But I'll fix that one day, and as soon as I do I'm going to find a hoop big enough to go through myself. I may even take a trip round the world.' He stretched his arms out either side of his wheelchair. 'Weeeeeeeee! Who needs to walk when you can fly!'

Finally, he took a deep breath, exhausted by his own enthusiasm. 'Now . . . do you think it's time we told the others what we've discovered?'

Polly and Tom nodded.

'Good, I'll round everyone up. You can have a game of Jumblupp while you're waiting,' he suggested, heading out of the door. 'You'll find a bag of Jumblupp pebbles on the worktop.'

Polly and Tom watched Seymour disappear down the ramp, then settled down to play Jumblupp. To Tom, the idea of using letters to invent words that didn't exist had seemed, at first, like an extremely silly thing to do. But he was starting to get the hang of it and had even beaten Polly a couple of times. He found the purple velvet Jumblupp bag and held it open for Polly, who closed her eyes and picked out eight small flat pebbles, each with a letter of the alphabet painted on it. The challenge was to use as many of them as possible to spell a new word, and to then say what that word meant. Scoring was equally simple: a point was awarded for each of the eight letters used, and up to a further eight points could be won depending on how closely the word matched its given meaning. Today they were both on top form, and after the first round had each scored the maximum sixteen points – Polly for her word 'pongtozy' meaning smelly feet, and Tom for 'lugdangl', meaning earring.

Now it was Polly's turn again.

She began picking another set of pebbles out of the bag. To her surprise the first three letters were Os.

'Tom! I'm not falling for that old trick,' she said, recalling how once when Tom wasn't looking she had swapped the real bag for one containing nothing but Os.

But when he held up his hands innocently she remembered that Tom never thought to trick anyone. It was the reason why he himself was always so easy to trick. So she continued, picking out P, X, E, M and N.

'Oh, that's so easy,' she said, quickly rearranging the letters. 'M-O-O-O-N-P-E-X. Mooonpex.'

'What does that mean?' asked Tom.

'Isn't it obvious?' she said, smiling mischievously. 'It means goodnight kisses – like this!'

She jumped forward, throwing her arms around Tom's neck as if to kiss him. Instinctively he lurched backwards, knocking the Jumblupp bag on to its side. A dozen pebbles spilled off the worktop and plopped into a bucket of Fizzle on the floor below, twisting and turning in the water as they sank slowly to the bottom. Eight of the pebbles settled face-up.

'Now look what you've done,' Polly teased him. 'You'll have to use those eight letters – it's the rule.'

Tom knew there was no such rule, but he fished out the eight pebbles anyway, drying them carefully with his handkerchief before placing them on the worktop.

Mmmm, he thought. S-K-O-N-T-G-N-I. What can I do with these?

He chewed his lip, moving the pebbles around for what, to Polly, seemed like an eternity. Finally, after several 'get-a-move-ons' from her he made his choice.

'G-O-S-T-I-N-N-K . . .'

'Don't tell me, let me guess,' interrupted Polly, putting on her best advertising voice. 'Get rid of the cheesy smell of pongtozy with Go-Stink Air Freshener.'

Tom shook his head.

'Nice try, Polly, but you're miles out. It's pronounced "ghost ink" – invisible ink for writing hidden messages. I reckon that's another sixteen points, don't you?'

But Polly didn't reply. Unknowingly Tom had given her an idea, and her eyes were now fixed firmly on the pebbles, as though they were trying to tell her something. Suddenly she jumped up and rearranged his letters.

'There! K-I-N-G-S-T-O-N. Kingston.'

Tom looked at her blankly.

'You do know where Kingston is, don't you, Tom?'

He blushed, shaking his head.

'It's the capital of Jamaica, silly. Don't you see, it's a hidden message from the Fizzle – it wants us to go there, too.'

'Well, I'll be a lobster's lunchbox.' Polly and Tom turned to find the Captain standing in the doorway. 'In that case I think we might be visiting Mamma Mango's Beach Café after all.'

Kruud Closes In

Shipley Manor's journey across the Atlantic Ocean wasn't at all as exciting as Polly had hoped it would be. There were no wild, raging storms to battle against, no wicked pirates to outwit or outrun, no fire-breathing sea serpents to capture and tame. Instead, day after day, the Fizzle spread itself flat in front of the house like a smooth tarmac road across a rough ploughed field, deflecting every wave in its path so that Shipley Manor's huge paddle-wheels could bite deep into the water and push it along as easily as if it were crossing a village pond.

'You'd think we could find at least one desert island with buried treasure on it,' she complained to Tom one day, only for him to point out that the Fizzle surrounding the house was already a kind of treasure, and that what they needed to find wasn't a desert island, but a way of keeping their promise to Hopper.

⚓

By now everyone on board knew about their mission, and had agreed that if the whole world 'Got the Fizzle' it would be a far happier place. After several days at sea the Captain was satisfied that were Shipley Manor and the Fizzle to become separated the house would be perfectly seaworthy, if somewhat slower. So all that remained was to spread the Fizzle around the world, although how they would do that was still a mystery. It seemed an impossible task, but Polly was certain the answer lay in Jamaica, because that's where the Fizzle, or so she believed, had told them to go.

Their arrival there was more exciting than the journey itself. The newspapers in England had been full of stories about Shipley Manor and the magic water surrounding it, and a floating country house was no less fascinating to the people of Jamaica. First to greet them was a small white motorboat. As Shipley Manor appeared on the horizon, it had come buzzing out of the harbour, spilling over with sightseers eager to gaze goggle-eyed at the centuries-old building and catch a glimpse of Polly, Tom and the Captain, whose faces had appeared on the front page of every newspaper from Tokyo to Timbuktu. The boat flitted and swooped around the huge stone house before being joined by another, then another, then dozens more, until soon an armada of white vessels surrounded Shipley Manor like a flock of hungry seagulls around a fishing boat.

They escorted Shipley Manor into Kingston Harbour, where a carnival of people had turned out to welcome them. As the Captain reversed the house against the quayside and lowered the drawbridge a steel band struck up and the local inhabitants crowded round to applaud and stare down into the famous magic water. At the front, motionless against the blur of brightly coloured streamers, flags and balloons that were being waved all around him, a stooped, grey-haired man waited patiently. Then, as the Captain emerged on to the drawbridge the man pulled a note from the pocket of his butler's uniform, and stepped forward to hand it to him. The Captain fished his reading glasses out of his dense black beard and, a few seconds later, turned smiling to Polly, who had stepped up beside him.

'Salivating seaslugs!' he bellowed to her above the music. 'Food! Someone called Sherman H. Kruud has invited us all to dinner tonight aboard his private yacht. How splendid!' He turned back to Kruud's butler. 'Please tell Mr Kruud that we'll be delighted to come.'

'Very good, sir – a car will pick you up at six,' replied the butler, and disappeared back into the crowd.

Just before six o'clock the crew of Shipley Manor stepped on to the quayside, each clutching a bottle of their favourite Fizzle cocktail to take along as a gift for their host. By now the crowd and steel band had departed, taking with them the sound of cheering and beaten oil drums, and leaving behind only the gentle clinking of yacht masts and lapping water. The Captain tipped his head back to sniff the warm, moist Caribbean air and catch the faint, appetising whiff of wood smoke drifting over from a nearby beach barbecue. Aaah, what mouth-watering local delicacies would Mr Kruud have in store for them tonight, he wondered – freshly cooked Caribbean seafood perhaps, or a Jamaican fruit platter, overflowing with star-apples and slices of ripe, succulent mango and papaya?

Like Slugbucket, who had polished his gardening boots and tied a bright red handkerchief around his neck, the Captain had spruced himself up for the occasion. Dinner was always special, doubly so when it was aboard a fellow seafarer's yacht, so he had decided to wear his naval uniform. As always, its silver buttons gleamed like mirrors, reflecting the rows of white lanterns strung like luminous pearls between the palm trees lining the harbour. He straightened his tie and turned to the young crewmate standing next to him. She was dressed entirely in brown, with her long hair coloured green and spiked high in all directions.

'Terrific outfit, Polly,' he said. 'I've never seen a walking palm tree before.'

Polly looked across at Tom, grinning proudly.

He smiled back. 'Just make sure you don't drop any coconuts on Mr Kruud's head,' he joked.

Then, as the harbour clock struck six, a white limousine rolled silently to a halt in front of them. Tom had been worrying how they would all fit into a car, but he needn't have. This car clearly had no idea where to end – it just went on and on, like a piece of chewing gum stretched almost to breaking point.

'Blimey,' said Slugbucket, scratching his head. 'So many bloomin' doors – 'ow are we s'posed ter know which one ter choose?'

But Polly had already chosen. 'Come on, you lot,' she called from inside, 'there's a seal in here serving drinks.'

The car sped them out of the harbour and began to twist and turn its way up into the mountains towards Kruud's private bay on the other side of the island. As the Captain and his companions settled back into their soft white leather seats to enjoy the journey, Arthur shuffled around the spacious cabin, offering glasses of Kruud Kola from a silver tray which remained perfectly balanced on his nose around even the tightest of corners. Polly nudged Tom in the ribs.

'Do you think it's glued on?' she whispered.

'I don't think so,' he whispered back, before realising that she was joking. Half an hour and, in Polly's case, three sickly glasses of Kruud Kola later, they rounded a bend on the other side of the mountains and caught their first glimpse of Kruud's yacht, lying like a white diamond in the clear turquoise ocean below.

At first Tom thought there might have been a mistake, because the yacht had no sails. Instead, it reminded him of the luxury liners he saw sometimes on the front covers of holiday brochures, advertising round-the-world cruises. 'Wow!' Polly pressed her nose up against the car window. 'Look at that! How rich can he be?'

At that moment the darkened glass in front of them slid down to reveal the same elderly manservant who had delivered their invitation. This time he was wearing a chauffeur's hat.

'Rich enough to own a string of private islands,'

he told her, 'and a special ship that can nibble each one into the shape of his choice. I hope that answers your question, madam.'

Then Tom realised.

'Does Mr Kruud have anything to do with the Kruud Kola Corporation?' he asked.

'That's right, sir. He owns it,' the man replied, 'along with the Kruud Oil and Gas Corporation, Kruud Chemicals . . .'

' . . . and the Kruud Motor Company?' asked Seymour.

'Indeed, sir. In fact, you're riding in a Kruud car now.'

'Well, I'll be a pirate's piggy bank,' said the Captain. 'Did you hear that, Calypso? We *are* honoured.'

The car continued winding down the mountainside, then followed the shoreline before turning on to the jetty. It clunk-clunk-clunked its way across the thick wooden planks to the end, where Moolah and Luka stood like palace guards either side of a steep gangplank.

'Do you think we should salute them?' Polly whispered as she and Tom climbed out of the car.

'Of course not,' he replied, only to see the Captain do just that as he followed the butler on to the gangplank.

The gangplank took them up to a hatch in the

side of the yacht and through into a wide oak-panelled corridor.

'Look at that, Polly,' marvelled Slugbucket, pointing to the floor. 'A red carpet – Mr Kruud certainly knows 'ow to treat 'is guests, don't he?'

The butler escorted them along the corridor in slow, deliberate steps, as though he might be trying to stop his highly polished shoes from squeaking. A pair of double doors stood open invitingly at the end.

'Mr Kruud is expecting you,' he said, ushering them through, before closing the doors quietly behind them.

Inside, the room was far bigger than any of them would have thought possible. It stretched the full width of the yacht and, from the rows of portholes lining each side, Tom reckoned that it was at least four decks high. A huge white glass chandelier hung down from the ceiling like a frothy waterfall frozen in mid-flow. Below it, in the centre of a large raised pool, as though it were floating in the middle of a milky-white sea, was something none of them would have expected to see in the Caribbean. Ever. Polly and Tom rubbed their eyes in disbelief.

'Freezing Fizzlefish!' said the Captain. 'An iceberg. It must be colder in here than I thought.'

Suddenly the tip of an overloaded pedal boat appeared from behind it.

'Howdy, folks, glad you could make it,' announced Sherman H. Kruud as he pedalled slowly into view, gently frothing up the milk behind him. The boat wobbled as he stretched over to the iceberg and broke off a huge chunk in his hand. 'Meringue anyone?'

After a puzzled silence, Tom was the first to remember his manners.

'Er, no thank you, Mr Kruud,' he replied politely.

'That's good, boy,' said Kruud cheerfully, taking a bite of the crisp white meringue before throwing the rest overboard. 'In that case you can use both hands to help me outta this damn pedalo.'

Tom stepped obediently to the edge of the pool and steadied the boat whilst Kruud climbed out, landing back on the wooden floor with a thump that sent clouds of meringue crumbs cascading out of his suit. He straightened his hat, then stepped forward to offer a sticky hand to the Captain.

'Welcome aboard my little boat,' he said, gripping the Captain's hand firmly before directing his guests to one of the large café-style tables dotted around the pool.

The Captain scanned the room out of the corner of his eye, hoping to spot a mouth-watering buffet tucked away somewhere. Instead, Arthur appeared balancing a tray of burgers on his nose.

'I got a real special treat for you tonight, folks,'

Kruud told them proudly. 'My own invention, comin' soon to a shoppin' mall near you.'

'Burgers?' asked Polly.

'Burgers! No siree. These ain't no ordinary burgers. These are "Alphabetiburgers". An' I do believe,' Kruud continued, peering down at the tray, 'that the one on top belongs to you.'

Polly leaned over and took the burger.

'The seeds on top are in the shape of a letter P,' she observed, turning it around in her hands.

'That's right – P for Polly. An individual burger for an individual customer. I'm about to open a worldwide chain of Kruud Alphabetiburger Bars sellin' monogrammed burgers. Twenty-six different varieties an' I won't even have to change the ingredients. Whaddya think?'

Polly took a huge bite.

'Ain't it the greatest thing since . . . well, Kruud Kola?'

Polly thought the burger tasted of soggy cardboard, but she nodded politely. It did have a special P on it, after all.

Kruud lifted the tray from Arthur's nose and placed it on the table.

'Help yourselves,' he told them. He was keen to get down to business. 'From what I've read about you in the newspapers we sure have a lot to talk about.'

The Captain picked up a burger with an H on top.

'We do?' he replied, nibbling the edge, cautiously.

'Sure we do. You see, I read all about how you looked after those city kids back in England. How you let them stay at Shipley Manor for their summer holidays an' taught them how to paint and cook and grow vegetables. In some ways it's a shame that Fizzle of yours dragged you away from such fine work.'

'That reminds me,' said the Captain, placing a bottle on the table, 'we thought you might like to try some.'

'That's mighty kind,' said Kruud, holding it up to the light admiringly, 'but if you don't mind I'll save it for later – I kinda like to share special treats like this with my children.'

'You have children?' asked Maggie, delighted. 'How many?'

Kruud smiled. 'Oh, thousands, ma'am – orphans from every war-torn, blood-soaked corner of the globe. I rescue 'em, take 'em in, feed 'em, clothe 'em and teach 'em skills just like you did back in England, Captain. My only regret is that so many of them continue to hate each other because they're from opposite sides. Fightin' and hatin' is all some of them have ever known, and there don't seem a damn thing I can do about it. Why, only a few days ago two of my favourites – Pepe and Paco – tried to kill each other right in front of me. I was mighty upset, I can tell you – mighty, mighty upset.

Kruud shook his head sadly. It was time to dangle the bait.

'If only I could make everyone get along together,' he sighed. 'But no matter how hard I try . . .'

Polly leaped to her feet.

'That's what the Fizzle does,' she said, excitedly. 'When you drink it you feel joined up with everyone, like you're part of one big family.'

'It does?' said Kruud, his eyes widening in mock surprise. 'Just by drinking it?'

'Yes,' she said, nodding, 'we call it "Getting the Fizzle".'

'Well, that's better than havin' to eat your way out of a meringue avalanche – it's the greatest discovery in history. Ya know, we have some serious do-goodin' to discuss here, folks. Are you aware that I own the Kruud Kola Corporation?'

'Your chauffeur told us on the way here,' said Tom.

'Did he also tell you that, by sheer luck, you're just a day's sailin' from my worldwide bottlin' plant on Dollar Island. Why . . . I could have this peace potion of yours bottled up and shipped out to all four corners of the globe in a matter of days. Whaddya say?'

The Captain coughed, embarrassed.

'It seems only fair to warn you that we're not really in a financial position to, er . . .'

'We haven't got two pennies to rub together,' Polly blurted out.

Kruud laughed.

'You don't need to worry about money, folks. What's the point of me drippin' in the stuff if I can't help good folk like you make the world a better place? Imagine – no more fightin', no more wars. What greater reward could I ask for than that? Don't worry, Captain, everyone's gonna "Get the Fizzle" – absolutely free of charge.'

Then a worry cast a shadow over Kruud's beaming face.

'Mind you,' he said, prodding the table, 'not everyone's gonna like what you good folk are doin'. If word gets out, every warmongerin' politician, every fire-breathin' fanatic, every pistol-peddlin', arms-dealin', missile-makin' businessman in the world will be lookin' for ways to stop you. They're not stupid, Captain. They'll quickly work out that if everyone in the world "Gets the Fizzle", the weapons in their factories will be worth about as much as a shipload of mushy meringues. Gee, they won't even be able to sell a pea-shooter, let alone a fleet of warships.' Kruud glanced suspiciously over his shoulder, then leaned closer. 'I expect they already know,' he whispered. 'Their spies are everywhere. In fact, I wouldn't be surprised if that no-good bunch of billionaire bandits – Ching an' Robovich an' Punjabootee – weren't even now arrangin' to send you and Shipley Manor to the bottom of the ocean in the hope that the Fizzle will follow you there.'

'Jumping jellyfish!' replied the Captain. 'I hadn't thought of that.'

'That's why I'd like to sail to Dollar Island alongside you,' Kruud continued. 'They won't dare attack you with me an' my boys close by.'

The Captain considered the offer for a moment, then shook his head.

'Thank you,' he replied, 'but we've always put our faith in the Fizzle and it's never let us down. I'm certain it will protect us from anything those scoundrels can throw at us. Besides,' he continued, 'I'm sure you'll need to go on ahead and make preparations for our arrival. The quicker we can bottle up the Fizzle the better.'

Kruud didn't look too happy about it, but he sensed that the Captain had made his decision.

'If you're sure, Captain. But don't forget they may also try to trick you. So trust no one, listen to no one an' whatever happens don't let anyone within' spittin' distance of Shipley Manor until you reach Dollar Island. And when you do, as sure as my name is Sherman H. Kruud, I'll see to it that the whole world "Gets the Fizzle". Halleeeeeeee-lujah!'

'Well, you two,' the Captain said, turning to Polly and Tom, 'it looks as though you might accomplish your mission sooner than you thought.'

'That's settled then,' said Kruud. 'Now . . . who's for another Alphabetiburger?'

⚓

Half an hour later, Sherman H. Kruud stood at the top of the gangplank waving goodbye with his enormous hat, as his guests set off in the limousine for their return journey to Shipley Manor. As its lights disappeared into the distance he turned round. His fish-breathed new business partner emerged from the shadows behind him, smiling.

'How was I?' he asked her.

'Ssssickeningly sincere, Sherman,' Pike replied. 'You nearly had me believing all that ssssave-the-world claptrap.'

A Warning

On the way back to Shipley Manor all was quiet apart from the sound of Calypso clapping her tiny hands together each time they passed another car. Tom knew he should be feeling happy. Instead, he was remembering something his father had said to him one night when he was struggling with some really difficult homework.

'The only place where achievement comes before effort,' he had said, placing a mug of hot chocolate on the table next to him, 'is in the dictionary.'

Even though his father's words hadn't helped Tom finish his homework any faster, they had made perfect sense to him. As he recalled those words now, it occurred to him that Shipley

Manor's silky-smooth passage across the Atlantic, their invitation to meet Mr Kruud and his offer to bottle up and distribute the Fizzle for them had all happened without any effort whatsoever. They hadn't really *achieved* anything. It had all been handed to them on one of Kruud's gold-rimmed plates. And that worried him.

He closed his eyes, hoping that Hopper might be able to reassure him. He hadn't been able to speak to Hopper for days. He counted backwards from ten. But nothing happened. He could sense that he was there, but it was as though his fellow Fizzler was permanently asleep. He closed his eyes and tried again. He wasn't sure, but this time he thought he could hear Hopper's voice. But it was different. Unusually, it kept fading in and out of his head like a radio channel with a weak signal. Could it be something to do with the mountains? Even when Hopper's voice did come through it sounded muffled and drowsy, as though he were fighting to stay awake. If so, perhaps he had something very important to say. Tom tried to shut out every other thought and concentrate on Hopper's voice. After a while he began to pick up a faint word here, a muffled word there – but they were always the same two words: 'Kruud' and 'trust'.

'That's good,' he thought, and kept listening. Then he heard a third word. He heard it only briefly, no louder than a whisper. But it was clear enough to make his heart sink. The word was 'don't'. Tom tried every combination, but no matter how he arranged the words only one order made sense. The message was clear: Don't–trust–Kruud.

Tom opened his eyes and leant over to Polly.

'We can't trust him,' he whispered.

'Who can't we trust?' she replied, loudly.

Everyone looked up. Tom pressed a finger to his lips and nodded towards the driver, who he knew might be listening.

'Ssssshhhh.'

Polly seemed to understand. Suddenly her voice was inside his head. They hadn't talked silently like this since being reunited at Shipley Manor.

'What do you mean?' she asked him.

'Hopper just told me not to trust Mr Kruud,' Tom replied in a whisper, even though he knew no one there except Polly could hear his voice. 'Didn't you hear him?'

'No,' said Polly, 'I was busy counting the cars going past.'

'I think he must be ill or something,' Tom continued, 'because his voice was so weak. But I'm sure he said, "Don't trust Kruud".'

'That's silly,' said Polly. 'Why would Mr Kruud offer to help us if he didn't mean to? Perhaps

Hopper's just talking in his sleep, or maybe a nurse has given him some funny medicine that makes him imagine things.'

'I don't know . . .' said Tom, uncertainly.

'Look,' Polly continued, 'the Fizzle has always protected us, hasn't it? So, if it isn't safe for us to go to Dollar Island, surely it will stop us from going there. And if it doesn't, if it actually *helps* us go there, then we'll know that we can trust Mr Kruud.'

'Maybe you're right,' said Tom. 'Perhaps the sensible thing to do would be to wait and see what the Fizzle does tomorrow.'

'Of course I'm right,' said Polly. 'Now, for goodness' sake stop worrying.'

She returned to her car-counting just as the limousine began its descent towards Kingston Harbour.

By the time she had counted to fifteen they had arrived back at the house.

Polly was first out of the limousine and skipped across the drawbridge. A large brown envelope marked 'PRIVATE AND CONFIDENTIAL' had been left propped up against the door. It was addressed to Tom. She picked it up and was about to hand it to him when suddenly she felt dizzy. She closed her eyes, only to find another word buzzing around inside her head. This time it was 'lies', and it was growing bigger, and louder, and pinker, and fluffier with every passing second, until it threatened to fill her head entirely.

So that was it. The envelope was a trick. She held it behind her back, whilst everyone filed past her into the house.

'I'll be in soon,' she explained. 'I'm just calling Nautipus.'

Then she ripped the envelope open. Inside was a scrapbook with a note attached to it. The note read:

Dear Tom

My great-grandfather, Hopper, has become quite ill. He fears that he may not always be able to communicate properly with you, and has insisted that I leave his bedside to deliver this urgent package. He says that you will understand what it means.

Yours sincerely

Scarlett Hawkins

Polly opened the scrapbook. Inside were dozens of newspaper clippings from around the world. They were of all shapes and sizes, a few even in languages that Polly couldn't understand, but they all had one thing in common. They were all about Mr Kruud – Kruud the polluter, Kruud the slave trader, Kruud the con man.

Finally, on the last page, written in spindly handwriting too large to ignore was the message:

Don't trust Kruud

Polly shook her head defiantly. Newspapers could lie – she knew that. And she wasn't about to let her shipmates be fooled. The scrapbook was a trick. She was as certain of that as she had been that they should all come to Jamaica. Mr Kruud had already warned them about such trickery, and now the Fizzle was telling her loud and clear that these stories were fake – nothing more than a pack of lies intended to put them off sailing to Dollar Island. The buzzing was growing louder now, pressing against the inside of her head. She clutched the scrapbook to her chest, wondering what to do with it. If she showed it to Tom, he'd probably believe every word and tell the Captain. What then? The whole trip might be cancelled. She couldn't take that chance. She slipped the scrapbook back into its envelope and stepped to the edge of the drawbridge. Glancing around to check that no one was watching her, she held the scrapbook out over the water. Then, just as the buzzing threatened to burst out of her head . . . she let go.

Rise of the Killer Coconuts

'What are you all staring at?' asked Polly.

The morning sun had just risen over the harbour and was streaming in long, lemony shafts through the portholes into the kitchen. The crew of Shipley Manor had gathered for an early breakfast and, for once, Polly had overslept.

'Well?'

'You're wearing pink,' said Tom, as though she might not be aware of it.

'I know I'm wearing pink,' she replied, yawning. 'So what?'

Tom paused, trying to make sense of what he was seeing.

'But . . . you hate pink. You won't even eat candyfloss because it's pink.'

He was right. Polly had never liked pink. And yet in the middle of the night she had woken up with a sudden, irresistible urge to rip up some old curtains and make herself a pretty pink dress.

'Well, obviously I've changed my mind, haven't I?' she replied, sharply.

The Captain and Maggie glanced at each other. They had noticed quite a few changes in Polly lately. For example, her refusal to eat fish, the mere thought of which she now claimed made her feel sick. Then there was her recent demand for more pocket money. And now, suddenly, she liked pink.

'Well, oi can't see what all the fuss is about,' said Slugbucket. 'You look roight noice in any colour, Polly.'

Polly threw her arms around his huge shoulders and kissed his stubbly cheek.

'Thank you, Slugbucket,' she said, taking her place next to Tom. 'I'm glad sssomeone around here has some fashion sssense.'

Tom turned pale and choked on his toast.

For a split second something in her voice terrified him. It was as though, for that moment, the girl sitting next to him wasn't Polly at all. He looked around the table, but no one else seemed to have noticed. They were more concerned with his coughing.

'Sorry . . .' he croaked, prodding his throat, '. . . crumb.'

The Captain stood up and tapped his mug with a teaspoon.

'Shipmates,' he said, 'in a few minutes Shipley Manor's paddle-wheels will be pushing us across the ocean to Dollar Island. The journey shouldn't take us more than a day, but Mr Kruud has warned us that there are those who might try to stop us reaching our destination. He may be mistaken, but we're not going to be taken by surprise. We'll take turns keeping lookout from the Crow's Nest and, if anyone approaches, Seymour has made sure that we have one or two surprises in store that should send them packing. And of course, anyone who picks a fight with us will find they have the Fizzle to contend with.'

'An' Polly brandishin' that Fizzlestick of 'ers,' said Slugbucket, adding quietly, 'Well, it scares me all roight.'

The Captain continued:

'All being well we should arrive at Dollar Island before dark and, by this time tomorrow, Mr Kruud will have started to bottle up the Fizzle.'

'I'm going to miss it,' said Polly. 'Can we keep some?'

'Just a few bottles, Polly. I know we're sitting on top of millions of gallons but there are a lot of people to share it with.'

'Around six and a half billion at the last count,'

Seymour added.

'Bloimey,' said Slugbucket. 'I 'ope Mr Kruud 'as enough bottles.'

Everyone stared at him. He had a point. How could anyone, even someone as rich and powerful as Mr Kruud, perform such a feat?

'Anything's possible,' Tom reminded them.

An hour later, Shipley Manor's paddle-wheels started to cut a foamy trail out of the harbour. Inside the Crow's Nest, Maggie and Calypso took the first shift as lookouts whilst Seymour brought Polly and Tom up to date with his latest inventions. Nothing much had changed since their last visit to his workshop. Buckets of 3F – Fizzle Flying Formula – still lay around the floor, but Tom did notice that some bottles on the shelf were now labelled '3F *Concentrate*'.

'I've made some progress with the flying formula,' Seymour explained. 'I thought that if we weren't going to have the Fizzle around for much longer I'd try to make a concentrated version that we could mix with ordinary water, rather like making a glass of blackcurrant squash from a capful of juice. It should work just as well as the stuff in those buckets there. Trouble is, I haven't tested it yet because we don't have any ordinary water on board, only Fizzle. This *does* work, though,' he announced proudly, lifting something from the worktop. 'I call it the Grand Xpander. It's a special kind of water pistol.'

He handed the contraption to Tom, who turned it around in his hands. It was made almost entirely from light reinforced metal, and its shape reminded him of a swordfish. At one end, something which resembled a tailfin had been padded so that it fitted snugly into Tom's shoulder. Handles were attached, like fins, to the top and bottom of the bulbous main body, each moulded so that his fingers would fit comfortably over them, and these allowed him to hold the device steady. At the front, protruding like the long snout of a swordfish, was a length of copper pipe, just wide enough for Polly to poke one of her fingers inside.

'I've made three of them,' Seymour told them. 'Each one hooks up to a hosepipe which pumps Fizzle up from underneath the house, so they never need to be refilled. Once you turn the pump on with this little switch, the water starts shooting out of the pipe.'

'We'd need more than water jets to fight off an attack, wouldn't we?' asked Tom.

'The Fizzle doesn't come out as a jet, Tom. It's trapped inside the main body at first, with more and more pressing up behind, squeezing it tighter and tighter until it's all set to explode. But it doesn't, at least not like the coffee filter did. You see, I fitted a special valve, like a trap door, halfway down the snout. A fraction of a second before the Fizzle explodes it opens up and fires out a droplet of condensed water, about the size of a marble. That reduces the pressure inside enough for it to shut again, but only momentarily, because the pressure builds up so quickly that it has to fire another one, then another, then another. Those little balls of condensed water leave the barrel ten times faster than any water jet. I call them Fizzballs.'

'Could they . . . kill someone?' asked Tom.

'No, of course not!' said Seymour. 'But they'll knock over anyone who gets in their way. You see, when a Fizzball leaves the barrel it's free to expand to its normal size, rather like a screwed-up crisp packet opening back out. So, by the time it reaches its target each one will have grown as big as an elephant.' Seymour chuckled. 'Imagine one of those hitting you – talk about "Getting the Fizzle"!'

Polly took the Grand Xpander from Tom and slotted the tail fin into her shoulder. Perfect. She couldn't wait.

'That's not our only defence, though,' said Seymour, taking it from her and putting it back on the workbench. 'Come with me.'

Leaving Maggie and Calypso to scan the horizon, Seymour led Polly and Tom on to the roof. Slugbucket was standing between the wind turbines at the stern, scratching his head with a spanner as he squinted at one of Seymour's scribbled drawings. Polly peered over his elbow, then took the scrap of paper and turned it the right way up, before returning it to him. Slugbucket's eyes lit up.

'So that's it – oi got it now. Thanks, Polly.'

He returned to his task, twisting, turning, tightening and tapping the final pieces of Seymour's latest creation into shape. Then he stood back to admire his handiwork.

'Finished,' he announced proudly, before returning his toolbox to the caravan.

'An old playground slide?' asked Tom.

'An organic aerial bombardment launching device,' Seymour corrected him.

The Captain stepped up behind Polly.

'Missile launcher to the rest of us,' he said.

'But we don't have any missiles,' Polly told him.

'Oh yes . . . we do,' said a slightly strained voice. Slugbucket had returned from his caravan with a marrow the size of a sofa clamped between his arms. 'I was saving it . . . for the Shipley Garden Show,' he explained from behind it, 'but I don't s'pose I'll be . . . enterin' that now – what with us bein' . . . thousands o' miles away an' all.' He lowered it down gently next to the slide. 'It's goin' a bit soft but no one else knows that.'

The Captain explained: 'I asked Slugbucket to harvest all the fruit and veg on Shipley Manor Estate just before the council arrived to take Polly and Calypso away. I thought we might be in for a long siege. We've got crates and crates of it lying around the place, far too much for us ever to eat.'

Polly didn't seem at all impressed.

'Fruit and veg?'

'*King-size* fruit an' veg,' Slugbucket reminded her. 'Reared on the finest slug juice my ol' slugpit could provide.'

'Why don't you test-launch one of those watermelons over there?' Seymour suggested.

So Polly retrieved one from a nearby crate and carried it back to the slide. She noticed that the slide had been suspended across the outer wall so that it hung out over the ocean. It was supported on top of the wall by a large swivelling bracket which, together with the old pram wheels attached to the bottom of its steps, allowed it to turn left and right. For aiming, thought Polly. She peered over the wall to discover that the slide had been lengthened, dropping steeply for two floors and, to her delight, looping the loop halfway down. At the bottom the slide curved upwards like a ski jump, so that anything leaving it would rocket back into the sky, passing through a metal barrel-hoop secured to the end by a large brass hinge. Beyond that, suspended on springs to keep it level, was a shallow metal tray full of Fizzle Flying Formula.

'Wow,' said Polly. 'What does the loop-the-loop do?'

'Nothing,' Seymour admitted, grinning. 'But I couldn't resist adding it. Who says organic aerial bombardment launching devices can't be fun?'

Polly heaved the watermelon to the top of the slide, then with a little push, sent it on its way. She watched it plummet downwards, rapidly picking up speed. As it approached the bottom it rolled over a small lever connected, via a series of cogs and pulleys underneath, to the hoop at the end. Immediately the hoop dipped forward into the tray of Fizzle Flying Formula, springing back just in time for the watermelon to shoot through it and emerge on the other side encased in a perfectly formed Fizzle bubble. The watermelon continued to rise fast over the ocean until it was about twice the height of the Crow's Nest. Then it glided to a halt and remained there, hovering.

Still Polly wasn't impressed – everyone knew that watermelons were made mostly out of water. Who'd be scared of that? she thought.

The Captain pulled a small wooden catapult from the centre of his beard and handed it to Polly.

'I bet you can't hit it first time,' he challenged her.

Polly frowned at him indignantly, before plucking an oversized Brussels sprout from a nearby crate and loading the catapult. Then she pressed her lips tight together, took aim and fired it into the sky. She scored a direct hit, as everyone knew she would, popping the bubble and sending the watermelon plunging towards the ocean. A second later it landed on a large piece of driftwood, smashing it in two with an enormous crack and sending both halves, plus the unfortunate seagull who had been taking a nap on it, flying high into the air. Polly smiled.

'Ouch!'

'Exactly, Polly,' said the Captain. 'This lot is quite enough to give anyone a nasty headache, wouldn't you say?'

She nodded, feeling rather foolish. Water was heavy. Water was dangerous. Water could break a boat in half. The Captain had told her a thousand times.

He clapped his hands shut briskly. 'So what else do we have to greet any unwanted visitors, Slugbucket?'

'Well, fer starters we got dozens o' huge

pumpkins I was plannin' ter turn into garden lanterns,' Slugbucket replied. 'I already started carvin' scary faces in 'em – look.' He lifted one of the pumpkins up to his face.

'Imagine that ugly mug 'urtlin' out the sky at yer – enough ter put the wind up anyone, oi reckon. We also got sackloads o' coconuts that Maggie bought in the market to make bird feeders before we set sail. Then there's crateloads o' rotten tomatoes, enough Brussels sprouts to fill a swimmin' pool, an' 'alf a dozen barrels brimmin' wi' extra-large cookin' apples. You name it, Cap'n, we got it.'

'You might as well have these, too,' Seymour said, lifting a large cake tin from his lap and handing it to the Captain. 'Edna's scones. She packs me off with dozens whenever I go away. They're always rock hard but I've never had the heart to tell her.'

'Your secret's safe with us, Seymour. Now, if that's everything, shipmates . . .'

'Not quite, Cap'n.' Slugbucket emerged from behind the caravan carrying a bulging sack over each shoulder. Tom followed him, dragging a third sack behind him at arm's length – well away from his clean trousers. Polly pinched her nose.

'Poo!' she said.

'That's roight, Polly – manure,' Slugbucket explained. 'We got 'alf a ton o' cow dung I was rottin' down ter fertilise me new vegetable patch. Let's drop this on 'em too, then at least if they sneaks on board we'll be able to smell 'em comin'.'

'Splendid idea,' agreed the Captain. 'Now let's gather everything together, shall we?'

An hour later, a vast armoury of fruit and vegetables had been gathered from around the house and assembled close to the slide, ready to be launched into the sky. And not a moment too soon. As Slugbucket dropped the final sack of rotten cabbages on to the floor, Maggie's voice boomed out from the Crow's Nest.

'Visitor west on the horizon,' she announced.

'I saw it too, over there,' Polly confirmed to the Captain, pointing.

The others scanned the horizon. Nothing.

'It was just a dot in that hazy bit in the middle,' said Polly. 'I was sure I saw it.'

Then suddenly, Tom heard a familiar sound.

'Look out!' he cried, ducking as the plane roared over their heads from behind, flashing past so low that the tip of its wing threatened to slice through the Crow's Nest, like a sword swiping the top off a candle. Then it rose, drawing a perfect semicircle in the sky before heading back down towards them, building up speed. Even above the roar of the engine Tom could hear the Captain's voice booming out.

'Under the caravan, shipmates, quickly.'

As the plane roared overhead a second time Tom threw himself to the ground, twisting to watch it pass just a few feet above his head. Although it was a seaplane with bright orange floats – quite different from the plane he'd encountered on his train journey a few weeks before – Tom noticed that its pilot was wearing exactly the same type of old-fashioned flying hat as the one who had waved to him. More puzzling still, having this time glimpsed it briefly, the pilot's face seemed strangely familiar. He jumped back to his feet and watched the plane circle high overhead. Next time, if he could hold his nerve and remain standing, he would get a far better look. Who was it? Had they been spying on him from the beginning? Once again the plane reached the top of its arc and began its descent, its wings scything through the air as it screamed towards him.

'Get under here,' the Captain bellowed to him. But Tom remained standing, as if his feet were glued to the ground. Polly covered her eyes with her hands as the plane roared towards him, drowning out her scream. 'Tommmm!'

A moment later, terrified, she opened a crack between her fingers and peeped through.

He was nowhere to be seen. Then she spotted

him, buried underneath the Captain, who had hurled him to the ground. Polly ran out from underneath the caravan.

'You stupid idiot,' she shouted at him. 'I thought you were supposed to be sensible. You could have been killed.'

'No, I couldn't,' he replied, getting back to his feet and dusting himself off. 'The plane didn't even come close – it passed right over the top. Look, it's almost disappeared.'

Sure enough, the plane was heading back to where it had come from.

The Captain looked Tom up and down to check that he was still in one piece. Then he breathed a sigh of relief as he watched the plane melt away into the haze.

'Well, if that's the best they can throw at us . . .'

But his words were cut short, as Polly tugged his sleeve and pointed back out to sea.

'Do you remember where I put my telescope, Polly? My eyes aren't quite as good as yours.'

'T for Tanzania,' she reminded him.

'Ah yes,' he said, pulling it out of his beard and extending it towards the horizon.

'Mmmm, I see what you mean.'

Sure enough, the plane had turned around and was coming back. But this time it wasn't alone. Below it, seven black rubber dinghies arranged in arrow formation were heading straight for Shipley Manor, white foam streaming behind them like jet trails. Though they were still some way off, the Captain could see that each boat carried two occupants, one at the stern, steering, the other crouched at the bow as if ready to pounce. They were dressed from head to toe in black wetsuits, their faces largely hidden behind tight rubber hoods. Inside each boat the Captain could make out lengths of rope, some with hooks attached, whilst watertight boxes stretched down both sides, no doubt containing weapons or even – if they intended to sink Shipley Manor, as Kruud had warned them – explosives. Finally, he could see that each boat carried a hand-held megaphone, presumably in order to demand his instant surrender. Well, they weren't going to get it. He snapped the telescope shut and pushed it back into his beard.

'To your posts, everybody,' he instructed. 'Seymour, you and Polly go up to the Crow's Nest and wait for my signal. The rest of us will begin loading up the bombardment.'

The Captain started sending the rest of the watermelons down the slide, each aimed at a slightly different angle. One by one they shot through the hoop and into the blue sky, rising to form a protective arc behind Shipley Manor's stern, like a row of giant beads. Tom and Slugbucket formed a chain passing the Captain the biggest and best of the ammunition – cratefuls of hard, spiky pineapples capable of puncturing the dinghies' rubber skins, an extended family of hideous looking pumpkins, enough head-cracking coconuts to stock a dozen country fairs and, of course, Edna's scones. Melons, marrows and other large missiles rose into the sky one by one. Others the Captain launched down thc slidc in long avalanches, the Fizzle bubbles closing only after the last stragglers had passed through, so that soon the sky became laden with squadrons of squashed tomatoes, great clouds of fluffy white cauliflowers and swarms of sweet potatoes.

'P'raps we should drop a few old cannon balls on 'em as well,' Slugbucket suggested when they'd finished. 'I found loads when I was clearin' out the cellar a few weeks back.'

The Captain shook his head.

'There's no need. You saw what the watermelon did to that driftwood. Just imagine what those coconuts will do. Rest assured, shipmate, when this lot starts raining down on them they'll know they're in a fight.'

Slugbucket peered down into the water.

'Well, at least the fish'll 'ave a roight ol' feast when this is over,' he observed.

The Captain looked up at the Crow's Nest. Polly, Seymour and Maggie, with Calypso strapped ready for action on her back, were in position. Polly aimed her Grand Xpander skyward at a large cluster of coconuts, then lowered it again and gave the thumbs up. They were ready.

The boats were approaching fast now, but had not yet crossed the line where seawater ended and the Fizzle surrounding Shipley Manor began. The Captain looked over the side, his hand resting on the hilt of his naval sword as he scanned the water for some sort of reaction from their uninvited guests. Friend or foe, he wondered – perhaps the Fizzle would tell them the moment they crossed that line. But the boats didn't cross it. Instead, they stopped short, rocking gently from side to side. One of the frogmen stood up and shouted something through a megaphone. But he was too far away to be heard, so the arrow edged closer, this time crossing slowly into the Fizzle. Well within earshot now, the man raised his megaphone a second time. But as he pressed it to his lips and began to speak, the Fizzle started to hiss, drowning out his words. So again, the boats edged closer. The frogman raised his megaphone a third time, only for the hiss to grow louder and louder the more he tried to make himself heard.

Then, suddenly, he was gone.

A Fizzball the size of a hippo had slammed into him and sent him flying backwards out of the boat. The Captain turned angrily to the Crow's Nest.

'Wait for my order, Polly – we don't know for sure whether they're friend or foe yet. We need to hear what . . .'

But it was too late. Taking a signal from their leader the boats were racing forward now, their powerful engines churning up a frenzy of white froth as they sped towards the house. As the first dinghy hurtled towards Shipley Manor's old stone walls the Fizzle gave the Captain the answer he'd been waiting for, erupting underneath it and flipping it upside down as easily as if it were tossing a pancake.

The Captain's eyes narrowed.

'Foe it is then,' he muttered, before raising his sword to give the order.

'Open fire!'

Collision Course

As the sea around them erupted in a hissing frenzy of whirlpools and waterspouts, Polly aimed her Grand Xpander into the sky. She unleashed a barrage of Fizzballs which thundered upwards like rampaging elephants, bursting every bubble in their path to fill the air with falling fruit and vegetables. Rock-hard watermelons fell like meteors, sending frogmen diving out of their dinghies. Others jumped for their lives as coconuts smashed down on their boats, cracking open their engines, and hard, spiky pineapples ripped deep gashes in their dinghies' rubbery sides. And whilst Polly was busy directing this bombardment on to their heads, the Fizzle was flexing its watery muscles and showing the frogmen quite clearly where its loyalties lay.

Giant frothy waves reared up in front of the dinghies like white horses, ready to crash down and crush them beneath their watery hooves. Other waves, high, flat walls of water, rose menacingly either side of them, before crashing together like cymbals, firing their occupants skyward like bars of soap clapped between slippery hands. Whirlpools appeared from nowhere, drawing dinghies into their gyrating grip only to fling them away like fairground passengers hurled from a runaway roundabout. Others sucked the boats deep into their centres, swirling them around in ever tighter circles before spitting them back out like discarded cherry stones. And no sooner had a dinghy escaped from one of the whirlpools than a waterspout would spring up underneath it, lifting it high on a column of water. There it would sit, helpless, whilst Maggie and Seymour took aim from the Crow's Nest and sent huge Fizzballs crashing into it, hurling the boat and its crew back into the ocean.

But the frogmen kept coming, righting their upturned boats and clambering back on board time after time, battered and bruised, to try and try again. So the battle raged on. As the sea turned red with barrel-loads of fallen berries, Tom and Slugbucket launched more and more reinforcements into the air for Polly to shoot down, and the Captain remained at the ship's wheel, twisting and turning Shipley Manor to keep the dinghies at bay behind the fury of white froth thrown up by its deadly paddle-wheels. Even the Fizzlefish appeared to join in the fight, leaping out of the turbulent waters to harry and distract and, occasionally, knock frogmen overboard with their blunt hardwood noses. But still the frogmen didn't give up. Each time the battle seemed lost, the mini-Armada would regroup and, in the face of overwhelming force, they would hurl themselves forward.

And then two of the dinghies reached the walls.

Suddenly a grappling hook appeared like a black hand over the wall in front of Tom, its clawed spikes digging like iron fingernails into the old stonework as a frogman began to climb the rope attached to it. Tom pressed his foot against the wall and pulled the hook as hard as he could to dislodge it. But the weight of the frogman held it tight. Far to his left, Slugbucket was busy lifting his prize marrow above his head, ready to hurl it down on the other dinghy. To his right in the conservatory the Captain was wrestling with the ship's wheel, trying desperately to keep Shipley Manor from capsizing as the Fizzle bucked and crashed all around it. Suddenly an arm reached over the wall and grabbed Tom's wrist. Tom punched it repeatedly in a frantic effort to break free. But the frogman's grip held firm. So he reached down and picked up a loose coconut from the deck, bringing it down on the frogman's hand with all the force he could muster. Still the grip held. Then the frogman's head appeared above the wall. He screamed something at Tom, but the hiss of the Fizzle seemed to be sucking all other noise out of the air and devouring it.

'Slugbucket! Captain!'

Neither of them could hear his calls for help, and any moment the frogman would be over the wall. Then Tom did something which he would never ever have imagined himself doing. He threw the coconut as hard as he could at the conservatory. It smashed straight through the glass at the back, sending jagged shards skidding across the floor to the Captain's feet. The Captain turned and saw him. Instantly he abandoned the wheel and rushed out, drawing his sword from its sheath as he ran. Tom was still battling to free himself from the frogman's outstretched arm when he reached him.

'Let him go, you scoundrel,' the Captain ordered, raising the sword above his head.

Tom shrank back, shutting his eyes in blind terror as the sun glinted on the razor-sharp blade.

Then suddenly the frogman was gone.

'Aaaaaaaaargh!'

Even above the din Tom could hear the frogman plummeting back into the ocean. He looked aghast at the Captain. Surely he hadn't . . .

'What a fuss!' the Captain shouted into his ear. 'I was only going to cut the rope. You'd better wind it up in case he decides to climb it again.' As the Captain ran back to his post, Tom untied the hook from the end of the rope and dropped it to the ground. Then, as fast and skilfully as any ranch hand, he coiled up the rope and slung it diagonally over his shoulder.

By the time he looked up a few seconds later, something had changed. The Captain was no longer at the wheel. Instead, he and Slugbucket were standing motionless on the deck, staring straight ahead of them at the biggest ship Tom had ever seen. Twice the height of Shipley Manor and longer than an airport runway, its bow was dropping open like a huge jaw as it approached them, ready to swallow Shipley Manor whole. Tom rushed inside the conservatory and yanked on the ship's wheel. First to port, then to starboard. The paddle-wheels didn't respond. Shipley Manor remained on a collision course. Suddenly the Captain grabbed his arm and pulled him out on to the balcony.

'There's nothing we can do,' he shouted. 'The Fizzle's taking us straight towards it, look.'

Tom leant over the side. Sure enough the Fizzle was smoothing a trail between them and the ship, tossing out of the way every dinghy that lay in Shipley Manor's path.

'We have to trust it, Tom. There's nothing else we can do now except join the others. Come on.'

By the time they reached the Crow's Nest the ship was almost on top of them, blotting out the sky, its huge gaping mouth ready to scoop them up. They watched helplessly from the walkway.

'First a few puny little dinghies then this monster. Now that's what oi call reinforcements,' said Slugbucket.

'It's nothing to do with the dinghies,' Polly corrected him. 'Look, there on the side – a big letter K. This must be the special ship Mr Kruud's chauffeur was telling us about.'

But it was too late. As she spoke, the Crow's Nest was plunged into semi-darkness as the Fizzle carried them into the ship's mouth like a spacecraft sucked into a black hole. Inside, dark metal walls rose up on three sides like rusting cliff faces stained with the filthy strata of past cargoes – mud, earth, sand and gravel. And then as the frogmen made one last, unsuccessful attempt to follow them inside, the huge jaw began to close behind them, gulping back millions of gallons of Fizzle which tipped towards them in a huge surge.

'Quickly everyone, inside!' ordered the Captain.

They dived for cover underneath Seymour's workbench just as the wave hit the stern. With nowhere to go but up, it rose, colliding with water forced up either side of the house. The giant plumes met each other above the Crow's Nest, exploding in all directions like a vast liquid flower suddenly bursting into bloom. Water crashed into the Crow's Nest, covering the workbench in broken glass and ripping the door off its hinges. As the jaw continued to close, the sound of crashing water echoed from side to side as it, like Shipley Manor, became trapped. The noise was deafening, but even with his hand clamped over his ears there was one other sound that Tom could hear. Hopper's words were faint, as if he were calling to Tom from inside a deep sleep. But there was no mistaking the urgency about them.

'Don't trust Kruud,' he said. 'For Archie's sake. Don't . . . trust . . . Kruud.'

Tom climbed out from under the desk, his stomach sick with uncertainty. He trusted the Fizzle, but he trusted Hopper too. Something wasn't right about this at all.

And then he saw it. A soggy piece of paper stuck to the window in front of him. If Tom had been looking for a sign there could have been none clearer. For there in bold letters, on a newspaper clipping ripped out of the scrapbook and pasted flat on the glass by the ricocheting water, was the headline:

KRUUD IN SECRET TALKS WITH
WEAPONS INDUSTRY

It was there for no more than a few seconds before the Fizzle washed it away again, but it was long enough for Tom to read the date above it, too. Yesterday. That was all the proof he needed. Kruud wasn't on their side at all. He knew that now. As the water began to settle and his shipmates emerged from beneath the workbench, Tom looked out at the huge jaw blotting out more and more of the sky as it closed behind them. In a few seconds they would all be trapped. He swallowed hard. With no time to explain, there was only one thing he could do, and he had to do it fast, before his shipmates could stop him.

He grabbed a bottle of Seymour's 3F concentrate from the shelf and rammed it into his pocket. Then he reached down and picked up the bucket of Fizzle formula and threw it at the open doorway. He scored a direct hit, soaking the whole area with the rubbery formula. Instantly it formed a thin, quivering film across the opening, filling the door frame as though it were a hoop.

'Don't do it, Tom, it's too dangerous,' Seymour

called, reaching out to grab him. But Tom was too quick.

'I have to,' he yelled, running towards the doorway. As he reached it he closed his eyes and launched himself through the gap before disappearing, head first, over the edge of the walkway.

Tom Jumps Ship

Polly screamed and ran outside, almost folding herself in two as she hurled herself against the railings to look for Tom.

'Tom! *Tom*!'

Seymour joined her moments later.

'Why are you smiling, Seymour?' she demanded angrily. 'It's a hundred feet down to the courtyard. Tom's probably broken every bone in his body.'

'I don't think so,' Seymour replied, his grin widening. 'Look.'

He pointed upwards. Tom was above them, suspended inside a perfectly formed bubble hovering just a few metres away. He looked nervous and wobbly, as though he were balancing on an invisible unicycle. But he was alive. Behind him, the huge creaking jaw had begun to close, blocking out the daylight to cast an early nightfall over Shipley Manor.

'I know I'm right,' he called back to them. 'I'll explain later, Polly.'

Then, as the long shadow crept menacingly over the house, Tom pushed his arms firmly towards the last band of sky.

The bubble responded unsteadily, wobbling from side to side as it approached the ever-decreasing gap. Then, with inches to spare on either side, Tom floated out into the blinding sunlight. As the jaw clunked shut behind him and plunged Shipley Manor into darkness, he raised his hands above his head, hoping the bubble would rise quickly before he could be spotted. Instead, it rose slowly and gracefully, like a hot-air balloon setting off on a Sunday afternoon pleasure trip. In a few seconds the seaplane would complete another circuit of the ship and the pilot would see him. Tom clenched his teeth in frustration. To his surprise the bubble jerked upwards. So he clenched his toes as well, and it rose a little faster. He discovered that the more he stiffened his muscles to make his body hard and straight, the faster he went, as though the Fizzle were rewarding his physical effort. So, as the seaplane turned towards him, Tom pushed his lips together, puffed out his cheeks like a weightlifter and tensed every muscle in his body until it was locked tight. Immediately the bubble shot upwards as though he'd pressed the top-floor button on a jet-propelled lift. Staying rigid was exhausting, like holding a block of concrete above his head. But in a few seconds he had risen so far above the seaplane that it looked no larger than a dragonfly skimming the surface of a pond, and he was able to let the air explode out of his lungs and then to relax. He lowered his aching arms so that the bubble slowed to a halt, then hung limp and still, as though he were floating face down in a swimming pool, to watch the events unfold beneath him.

By now Kruud's ship had turned around and was ploughing a deep white furrow towards Dollar Island. The two remaining dinghies hadn't given up the fight, and were still attempting to reach Shipley Manor, vainly throwing themselves at the ship even though its sides were hundreds of feet higher than their ropes could reach. From Tom's height they looked no more dangerous than a couple of tadpoles trying to bite a whale. The Fizzle seemed to agree with him. Kruud's ship had gulped down some of the magic water when it swallowed the house, but the majority of it remained outside, following Shipley Manor as it was carried away inside the ship's belly. But it was no longer bothering with the dinghies it could so easily overturn. Instead, it let them wear themselves out until eventually, exhausted and low on fuel, they turned back to pull their floundering comrades out of the water. Tom watched the seaplane land briefly before leading its bruised and battered army away with a survivor clinging to each float. In a few seconds, as quickly as they had arrived, Shipley Manor's attackers had melted back into the horizon. Tom continued to hover, his head full of questions. He liked things to make sense, but nothing seemed to today. Kruud was up to no good, he was certain of that. Yet the Fizzle had allowed Kruud's ship to swallow Shipley Manor without protest. Perhaps it was simply protecting them from an even greater danger, because there was no doubt it had defended them ferociously against the dinghies, almost as though the future of the world depended on it. Something else puzzled him, too. Each time the Fizzle flipped a dinghy high into the air it had frothed up to catch the falling occupants in soft, foamy hands on their return to earth. But despite doing this with the same lightness of touch with which a father might catch a baby, the attackers had still received thorough dunkings. They had also been hit by a relentless barrage of Fizzballs fired from the Crow's Nest. So why had none of them appeared to 'Get the Fizzle'? They must have swallowed gallons of it during the fight. Neither could they have been in any doubt that anything was possible, having witnessed the awesome display of magical power directed against them. Yet all those who had managed to clamber, choking and spluttering, back on board a dinghy had renewed their attack on Shipley Manor more fiercely, if anything, than before. Why hadn't any of them stopped fighting? Tom shook his head, mystified.

The ship had shrunk to a dot now. He would follow it, but first he had to warn Polly about Mr Kruud. He closed his eyes and counted backwards from ten, imagining that he was talking to her. When he reached three he heard Polly's voice.

'Tom? Where are you? Are you all right?'

'Polly, you have to listen to me. Hopper was right. You can't trust Mr Kruud. He doesn't want everyone to "Get the Fizzle" at all. I've seen proof. You've got to tell the Captain.'

'But Mr Kruud *rescued* us, clever clogs,' she replied, 'and the Fizzle helped him, remember?'

'He didn't rescue you, Polly – well, maybe he did – but he's kidnapped you as well. I can't explain it. All I know is that you've got to escape.'

Polly didn't reply.

'Polly, what's wrong?'

Still she didn't answer.

'Polly, *Polly*!'

But she'd gone. The connection was lost. There

was nothing Tom could do now except follow the ship to Dollar Island. He pushed his arms in its direction, then crossed his fingers for luck. Instantly the bubble spun out of control. He relaxed and slowed to a halt. Clearly this was going to be harder than he thought. He tried again, stretching his arms out with his hands pressed flat together in front of him. Then he tensed his muscles gently and began to move forwards. This time he veered off slowly to the right. Perhaps his right arm was a fraction longer than his left because of all the bowling he did in school cricket matches. He didn't know. Either way it was clear that, whilst launching himself up into acres of sky had appeared easy, steering a straight and level course across the ocean was going to be as painstaking as threading a needle. Because the faster he tried to go, the more each tiny movement of his body was magnified. A misaligned elbow and the bubble would lurch drunkenly from side to side, a slight crook in the knee and it would duck and dive like a runaway rollercoaster. He couldn't even scratch his nose without flipping over on to his back. Holding a steady course was possible, but until he mastered control over the bubble it would be slow, plodding work, like walking along a tightrope.

Then he remembered that Hopper had

promised to give him any skill he needed to complete his mission. Well, right now he needed to know how to fly, and although the bubble wasn't an ordinary aeroplane he felt sure Hopper's flying skills would help him. He closed his eyes and began counting, imagining himself once again flying over rooftops. As he blocked out all other thoughts the rooftops became sharper, more colourful, and suddenly no longer just in his head but outside too. He was flying over them now, able to pick out every detail – the different coloured tiles on the rooftops, odd socks hanging out to dry on washing lines and in the distance a windsock, the door into Hopper's mind. If only he could fly like this in real life, he thought. Well, maybe Hopper could help him. He reached the windsock and hovered in front of it like a humming bird at the mouth of an orange flower.

'Hopper,' he called, 'can I come in?'

There was no answer.

'Hopper,' he tried again, 'I need your help.'

Still there was no reply. Perhaps Hopper was asleep, or too ill to answer. What would Hopper want him to do? That was easy – he would want him to complete his mission. So Tom flew inside. halfway down the billowing orange tunnel he noticed something strange. A smell. It took him a few seconds to realise what it was, but the moment he emerged inside Hopper's mind and floated down to the floor of the aircraft hangar it became obvious. Fish. The whole place reeked of rotting fish. Tom didn't waste any time. He put his sleeve over his nose and headed straight for the basement. The door was gaping wide open. That was even stranger. Hopper would never leave a door like that. He was tidy, like Tom. Nervously he descended the steps and flipped on the light. As the long room flickered into life Tom suddenly felt sick. The room had been ransacked. Sweet-jars lay smashed on the floor, their spewed-out contents – everything from Bonbons and Black Jacks to Pink Shrimps and Pear Drops – strewn lifelessly among the jagged glass like dead bodies on a battlefield. Other jars lay empty on the shelves, their contents missing without trace. Tom tiptoed through the carnage, trying not to tread on any of the sweets and, occasionally, picking up an unbroken jar to place it back on the shelf. Some of the first jars were untouched, but the further he walked the worse the mess became. Finally he reached the jar marked 'Flying' which, when Tom had seen it last, had been full to the brim with sherbet flying saucers. Now it was empty. Someone had eaten not just one of the sweets – they had devoured the lot. His disappointment turned to disgust when he realised what that meant for Hopper. When he wakes up, he thought, staring angrily into the empty jar, he won't know how to fly a plane any more. All that knowledge has been stolen from him.

Who could have done such a wicked thing? Obviously not Hopper himself. And surely not Polly. It was true she could leave a room looking like a tornado had hit it, but she would never steal anything. Only one explanation made sense to Tom. There had to be another Fizzler. Someone who had been lurking around all this time, concealed from the rest of them. He clutched his head, horrified. Had they been listening to his conversations with Polly and Hopper all along? Could some phantom Fizzler even now be wandering around inside his own mind? Or were they still there in Hopper's, hiding, preparing to pounce on him? Tom held his breath and listened. Nothing. The only sound he could hear was that of his own heart pounding.

Suddenly a deafening shriek pierced the silence: 'Aaaargh!' Tom jumped, knocking the empty sweet-jar off the shelf. As the glass shattered against the hard stone floor he opened his eyes. He was back in the bubble, staring down at the ocean spread out like an endless silver-blue carpet thousands of feet below him. For a moment he forgot he was safe inside and panicked, flapping his arms and legs about in a desperate search for something to hold on to. The bubble responded to every frantic movement, twisting and turning him around like a teddy bear in a tumble dryer, until he had no idea which way was up, and which was down. After a few seconds, when he noticed that the ocean hadn't come any closer, he remembered where he was and stopped thrashing around. He relaxed and took some long, deep breaths to settle himself and the bubble. Then he heard the shriek again. Only this time he knew what it was. A seagull. Relieved, he glanced sideways, only to find that the bird, with a rather surprised-looking fish clamped sideways in its beak, was heading straight for him. He froze like a rabbit in front of a car's headlights, unable to do anything except close his eyes and wait for the pop.

But it never came. When he opened them a second later he saw that the seagull had veered off sharply towards Dollar Island, leaving the bubble untouched. Taking supper home for the family, thought Tom, suddenly wishing he was back in Shipley with his father. He watched the seagull glide away, occasionally turning its head to look back at him as though it were expecting him to follow. Perhaps he should. Dollar Island was a long way off and he could do with the company. Besides, he thought, slowly extending his arms to edge the bubble forward, who better than a seagull to give him his first flying lesson?

Kola City

Sherman H. Kruud and Venetia Pike peered down from the viewing platform. Sprawled below them, in the massive hollowed-out cavern deep inside the volcano, Kruud's bottling factory resembled a miniature city at the height of rush hour. Crates of bottles, some clear, others filled with dark brown Kola, rose in tall, thin stacks like glass skyscrapers, their top floors shrouded in wisps of steam which hung in the air like low cloud. At their feet, boxes of Kruud Kola labels, stacked in huge blocks, squatted square and solid like concrete office buildings. Connecting them all, a network of rumbling conveyor belts transported an endless stream of bottles like slow-moving traffic along busy roads, alongside which a thousand filthy, threadbare children stood hunched together like weary commuters waiting for a bus, labelling, capping and packing the bottles at different stages in their journey. Behind them, bad-tempered bamboo-masters patrolled between junctions, screaming orders above the din of the machines and swishing their canes menacingly as they sought to keep the traffic flowing smoothly. Others operating remote controls gazed upwards. There, beneath a web of cables strung across the ragged rock ceiling, rusty mechanical grabbers moved up and down on long chains like an invading army of giant metallic spiders dangling on their threads, picking up and delivering crates and boxes around the factory.

Kruud turned to Pike and cupped his hands around his mouth.

'Welcome to the Kola capital of the world, ma'am,' he shouted.

'Very impressive, Sherman,' she assured him, 'and all hidden inside a volcano – how very original.'

'It's the biggest bottling factory on the planet,' he continued proudly. 'Fifty million bottles a day, and hardly anyone knows it's here.'

Pike nodded impatiently.

'You promised to show me the Fizzle storage tanks,' she reminded him.

'All in good time, ma'am, all in good time.'

He reached behind him and lifted a silver triangle and its steel striking rod from a hook on the wall.

But he didn't play the instrument straightaway. Instead, he closed his eyes and began gracefully to waft the slim metal striker from side to side like a baton, conducting the low, rhythmic chanting of the children as they carried out their tasks: 'Label straight, cap on tight . . . label straight, cap on tight . . . label straight, cap on tight . . .'

He floated up on to his toes, light with pleasure.

'Don't you just luuurve the sound of money being made, ma'am?'

'Get on with it, Sherman!' she snapped.

He opened his eyes and grinned at her.

'You ain't got no soul, Venetia,' he told her – quite accurately, of course. Then he tapped the triangle with a gentle flick of his wrist, sending out a sharp, high-pitched 'ting' which cut through the factory hubbub like an arrow through fog. Immediately the bamboo-masters punched the red 'STOP' buttons on the sides of the conveyor belts and they fell silent. Kruud's ragged workforce looked up.

'Now listen,' he announced. 'I got some mighty important guests arrivin' here soon, an' I don't want 'em castin' their eyes on a bunch of lazy, lice-ridden low-lifers like you. So I want you outta here and into your oil drums until they're gone.'

A thousand young jaws dropped open. Time off. It was unheard of.

'An' if you think this means I'm goin' soft, be warned. If my visitors catch even the tiniest, itty-bitty glimpse of you, if they so much as sniff you, you'll find yourself "walkin' the runway". So, unless you fancy an amble down alligator alley,' he continued, pinching an invisible pea between his fingers, 'I suggest you squeeze yourself up reeeal small inside those oil drums of yours an' stay there, quiet as mice, till you're told to come out. Have I made myself clear?'

'Yes, Mr Kruud.'

'Whaddya say?' he replied, cupping his ear.

'Yes, Mr Kruud.'

'Good. Now, the last one outta here eats fish guts . . . for a week!'

Instantly, a thousand children surged towards the narrow exits, each trying to push their way through ahead of the next. No one wanted fish guts for tea, and as the rush became a crush those furthest from the doorways began to fight and claw their way in front of each other until, finally, the smallest, weakest child was forced to the back. Kruud watched his workforce respond to his command with a mixture of pride and disgust.

'Little savages,' he tutted, shaking his head. Then, as the factory cleared and the last remaining child was led away, barefoot and sobbing, by an unsympathetic bamboo-master, Pike and Kruud descended to the factory floor.

'Your carriage awaits, ma'am,' said Kruud playfully, helping Pike into a nearby golf buggy. 'Hang on tight!'

He tooted the horn and they set off, weaving their way through the bottle-lined boulevards of Kola City towards the far side of the factory – past the black, grease-covered engines which powered the conveyor belts, past the pumps which filled the bottles as they rattled along on them, past the towering, Kola-filled tanks waiting to be drained of their sickly-sweet contents. Eventually, as they neared the end of their journey, four new storage tanks loomed up in front of them, awaiting Pike's inspection. The buggy hummed to a halt.

'Had 'em shipped in specially from one of my oil refineries,' Kruud told her. 'Each one holds fifty million gallons.'

Pike climbed out of the buggy and removed one of her pink stiletto shoes. Hobbling from tank to tank she hammered the side of each one hard with the heel. The dull, hollow clunks which echoed back showed her they were empty. But she knew they wouldn't be for long. From the front of each tank a flexible metal pipe, about the width of her shoulders, curved like a giant elephant's trunk down to the floor, as though it might be sucking up the concrete.

'The pipes lead through to the cave below,' Kruud explained, watching Pike step back into her shoe. 'As soon as Shipley Manor sails into it the pipes will suck up all the Fizzle until the tanks are full. Then it's ours, and there won't be a damn thing Captain Shipley or anyone else can do about it.'

'And that one?' Pike asked, pointing to a fifth pipe which led directly into the ceiling a hundred feet above.

'That's nothing, just a ventilation shaft,' he told her.

Pike smiled, satisfied that everything was going according to plan.

'And you think Captain Shipley and his merry band of misfits will go along with it all?'

'Sure they will. I'll just tell 'em we're going to start bottling the Fizzle as soon as these tanks are full. I've even had some fake Fizzle labels printed – look.'

He led her to the nearest stack of boxes. On the outside of each box a label had been stuck to indicate its contents. Pike peered closely at the dummy label. 'Fizzle,' it read, 'for that fabulous family feeling'.

'Of course we've printed some in Chinese, Arabic, Spanish, every language you can think of.'

'Very convincing,' Pike complimented him, picking at the corner with a talon-like fingernail. As she suspected, there was a Kruud Kola label hidden underneath.

'That's what's really inside the boxes, of course,' Kruud told her. 'A billion or so – just our normal monthly supply.'

For a few blissful moments, Pike imagined the Captain's face when finally he realised that he'd been tricked.

'Do you know what the ssssweetest thing in the world is, Sherman?'

Kruud shrugged his shoulders. 'Meringue?' he suggested.

'Revenge,' she corrected him. 'Ssssettling old sssscores.' She smoothed the corner of the label back down. 'And how's our deal with Robovich and the others going?'

Kruud smiled confidently.

'I've begun negotiations,' he confirmed. 'I sent each of them a sample bottle to test on their staff. Once they know Shipley Manor's arrived and we've got the Fizzle sealed up, they'll have no choice but to co-operate, unless they want to see their business empires disappear faster than a volcanologist down an alligator's throat.'

'Sssplendid.'

Kruud looked at his watch. Shipley Manor would be with them soon. 'I've arranged for a couple of my boys to drive you back to the villa. You can stay there out of sight whilst I go down to the cave to welcome our guests. I don't want them to suspect anything until we have every drop of Fizzle safely sealed inside those tanks. After that, we'll let the dopey do-gooders sail happily off into the sunset. By the time they realise the world isn't awash with bottles of their precious Fizzle there won't be a damn thing they can do about it.'

He turned to leave.

'One last thing, Sherman.'

Kruud turned back, just as Pike's thumb and forefinger pressed lightly but expertly into his neck. Instantly his knees buckled and he sank to the floor, arms hanging limp at his side. She pressed her nose up against his, staring deep into his eyes for any hint of betrayal.

'You wouldn't even conssssider double-crossing me as well, would you, Sherman?' she hissed, menacingly.

He shook his head, pressing his lips together to avoid the foul fishy breath, which was threatening to knock him unconscious.

'Half of *everything*, remember?'

He nodded enthusiastically, his bloodshot eyes

bulging as his face began to swell up like a purple balloon.

'Good, I'm glad we underssssstand each other.'

She released her grip and Kruud crumpled forward on to his elbows, gasping.

'You sure know . . . how to . . . impress me, ma'am,' he said eventually, climbing back on to his feet and swiping the dirt from his knees with the rim of his hat. 'Where the hell d'ya learn ter do that?'

'Oh, it's just a little sssskill I "acquired" from an old friend,' she called back, heading for the exit. 'With a little help from the Fizzle, of course.'

Alligator Alley

Polly opened her eyes and looked up. The Captain and Maggie were sitting either side of Calypso on the edge of her bunk. 'Welcome back,' said her mother, slipping a thermometer into Polly's mouth. 'You fainted. We've been quite worried about you.'

'Are we there yet?' asked Polly, dropping her hand out of the bunk to stroke Nautipus, who had just come in to investigate.

'Soon,' her mother replied, checking her watch. 'We think we can hear the ship's engines slowing down.'

'Have I missed anything exciting?'

'Not unless you count Seymour and Slugbucket rushing around with those two Fizzle-breathing slugs in their pockets,' Maggie replied, retrieving the thermometer. She examined it under the bedside light, nodding her approval before pushing it back into the Captain's beard. 'They've been trying to find out whether they can talk to each other from opposite ends of the house.'

'I don't suppose you have any idea, do you?' the Captain asked.

Polly closed her eyes and started to count backwards. Suddenly she felt trapped and breathless and a bit, well, sluggish.

'I can't tell,' she said, eventually, 'but they're pretty fed up being stuck inside those matchboxes, that's for sure.'

She looked around the room.

'Where's Tom?'

'We were hoping you might be able to tell *us*, Polly,' the Captain said. 'We thought you two might have been . . . talking.'

Then Polly remembered what had happened.

'We were. He was trying to tell me something about Mr Kruud. But every time I tried to listen to him, words started buzzing around inside my head, telling me to ignore him. And the more I tried to listen the louder and bigger the words grew, until they filled my head so that I couldn't think or do anything.'

'Including stand up,' her mother observed.

'It's the Fizzle,' Polly continued. 'It keeps telling me that Tom's being tricked.'

'Tricked?' asked the Captain.

'Into thinking Mr Kruud is a crook,' Polly explained.

'What a nautical numbskull!' said the Captain. 'Surely he knows that the Fizzle wouldn't have brought us here if that were true.'

'That's what I keep telling him,' said Polly, 'but he won't take any notice. And now he says he's seen proof.'

Suddenly she sat up. 'Listen.'

'But . . .'

'Schhh . . .' Polly held her finger to her lips.

'This is silly, Polly,' whispered her mother. 'I can't hear anything.'

'Exactly – that's because we've stopped,' said Polly, leaping out of bed and grabbing her Fizzlestick. 'Come on. We have to find Tom.'

The crew of Shipley Manor gathered under the dim lights of the conservatory. The Captain busied himself at the controls, slowly turning the starboard paddle-wheel to rotate the house until it was ready to greet the outside world head on. Then they waited.

Suddenly there was a loud clunk, and a dazzling

white line cracked the darkness. Light flooded in, soaking the top of the Crow's Nest before spreading down the building stone by stone, floor by floor, as the huge jaws creaked open. Polly shielded her eyes, peering through the cracks between her fingers as the mouth of the cave revealed itself in front of them. Around and above it, Kruud's volcano rose dark and sheer, blocking out the night sky. In front, light spilled out over the Fizzle, spotlighting the billions of sparkling bubbles dancing on its surface, as though they were performing on a silvery stage. The Fizzle was glad to be there. Polly could tell. The Captain sent her rushing up to the Crow's Nest with orders to warn him if it was about to hit the top of the cave mouth. Then, gently, he turned the paddle-wheels, and Shipley Manor left the sanctuary of Kruud's ship to make the short journey from one mouth to another. The Fizzle pushed into the cave ahead of it, forcing the plain seawater out at the sides as it flooded in through the centre. Then Shipley Manor followed it in. Polly ducked as the Crow's Nest passed under the top of the cave mouth with no more than a couple of inches to spare, but once they were inside the cave opened up high and wide. A long wooden jetty stretched the length of one side on which, flanked by Moolah and Luka, Kruud stood waving his huge white stetson hat in extravagant greeting. The Captain reversed Shipley Manor against the jetty, then lowered the drawbridge. Polly flew down the helter-skelter leading down from the Crow's Nest and was first to emerge from the house, followed moments later by the others.

'Glad you could make it, folks,' Kruud called out, bouncing over the wooden planks to meet them. 'I hope you're not mad at ma boys for givin' you a ride back there. I told 'em you might need a little help.'

'We most certainly did,' replied the Captain, shaking Kruud's hand gratefully. 'Even with the Fizzle helping us, those scoundrels just wouldn't give up. I've never seen such desperate determination.'

'Well, you're all safe now, that's what matters,' said Kruud.

The Captain shook his head. 'I wish that were true,' he replied, grimly. 'Unfortunately, we've lost Tom.'

'You mean he fell overboard?'

'Not exactly,' the Captain replied. 'He, er . . .'

'He flew away,' said Polly.

'Don't tell me he suddenly sprouted wings?' Kruud joked, shuffling along flapping his arms like a penguin.

There was an awkward silence – surely everyone

knew that penguins couldn't fly? Besides, it was hardly something to joke about.

'Not quite,' Seymour began to explain. 'You see, I've developed a formula which . . .'

'An' why would the boy do a damn fool thing like that?' Kruud interrupted.

Polly was first to answer.

'Because he thinks you're a crook,' she told him.

The Captain looked at her sternly.

'Well, he does! But it's all right, Mr Kruud,' she added, 'the Fizzle trusts you and so do we.'

Kruud bit his lip thoughtfully. He didn't like troublemakers. Just bad losers most of them. This one would have to be found and kept out of the way. Kruud excused himself and returned to the jetty for a few seconds. He spoke quietly to Moolah and Luka, who left quickly through a side door. Then he returned to his guests on the drawbridge.

'I've sent ma boys off to mount a search,' he assured them. 'If your misguided young friend is hidin' on the ship or somewhere here on Dollar Island we'll find him. In the meantime, I'll let the coastguard know he's missing, an' as soon as it's light we can get back out to sea an' start lookin' for him. But don't forget, Captain, until we have the Fizzle stored safely away you're all in terrible danger. If it follows you outta this cave your attackers will strike again, only this time they'll hit you twice as hard, an' twice as fast. So I suggest we start gettin' the Fizzle into those bottles right away.'

The Captain hesitated. It was all happening so fast. Although everything was as they'd agreed, the Fizzle was so precious. Was there *any* possibility that Tom could be right about Mr Kruud? He had always been so reliable.

'I tell you what,' Kruud continued, in his most convincing nothing-to-worry-about voice. 'As soon as we've started suckin' it up into the bottlin' factory I'll give you a guided tour, just to prove that Tom's suspicions are unfounded. I'm sure you'd like to see for yourself.'

That was enough to reassure the Captain. He nodded his agreement. Kruud smiled and signalled to another of his bamboo-masters perched high up on a walkway above the cave entrance. The tall, gangly youth turned obediently to a control box set into the rock and punched a green button. Immediately, a giant security grille began to slide down over the mouth of the cave, as though it were protecting the entrance to an expensive jeweller's shop.

'It's for your own safety,' Kruud explained as its bottom edge dipped beneath the surface of the water. 'It'll keep any mischief-makers out but let the Fizzle flow in through the holes. There's still plenty queuin' to come in by the looks of it.'

Then he turned to the other end of the cave, where five silvery-grey pipes rose up like cathedral columns from the surface of the water, before disappearing into the cave roof far above. Standing on the jetty alongside them, another bamboo-master awaited Kruud's signal. When it came he grasped the heavy lever set into the wall with both hands, and pulled it down. Moments later a loud sucking noise, which reminded Polly of Fizzle Cocktail being drained from the bottom of a glass, echoed around the cave as the pumps began their work. At the same time she noticed Fizzle starting to flow into the cave to replace the water that was being sucked upwards through the pipes. There was no turning back now. Operation 'Get the Fizzle' had begun. If only Tom were there to see it . . .

In fact, Tom wasn't very far away at all. Even though he hadn't managed to keep up with the seagull, he'd zigzagged his way slowly to Dollar Island behind Kruud's ship, whose distant lights had become easy to follow as night fell. He was hovering far above it now, having watched Shipley Manor sail out of it and into the cave. What should he do next? Several times he had tried to talk to Polly, but each time he'd been unable to, as though, like Hopper, she was asleep or unconscious. He had to know that she was safe, but if he followed Shipley Manor through the cave mouth he'd be spotted straightaway. Even if he wasn't, even if he could get close enough to the Captain to talk to him, how could he make him believe that the Fizzle had made a mistake and that Mr Kruud couldn't be trusted? There was only one sure way. He would have to discover what Mr Kruud was up to, then take proof to the Captain. But first he had to land. He knew that until Seymour improved the formula the bubble would burst as soon as it touched the ground, leaving him to fall the rest of the way. It would only be a short drop, but he couldn't risk twisting his ankle. He would need to land somewhere open and flat. Then, he remembered Kruud boasting that he owned an aeroplane. So he turned his eyes away from the glare of the cave mouth and scanned the darkness which lay over the rest of the island. Gradually, as his eyes readjusted to the moonlight, he found what he was looking for. A runway. Perfect.

He guessed correctly that the lights twinkling at the far end of the island belonged to Kruud's villa. Perhaps he would find the evidence he needed there, but first he wanted to check that Polly and the others were safe. And that meant finding another way into the cave. Tom hovered above the runway, watching the rippling moon reflected in patches of water on either side, looking and listening for any signs of life. But all was still. Good. He would land just a hundred metres or so from the gate at the end, which was set into a high security fence surrounding the volcano. Beyond it, alongside the dirt track leading from the gate, he could see hundreds of oil drums lined up in orderly rows, like a vast metal army awaiting inspection. Behind them were several dimly lit tin huts, their roofs reflecting the cold, silvery-blue moonlight, each about the same size as Slugbucket's old tool shed on the Shipley Estate. Tom crouched down inside the bubble and it descended slowly. A few feet above the runway he straightened up into a jumping position, keeping his knees slightly bent but stretching his arms out wide to balance himself. The bubble slowed almost to a halt. Just a few more inches . . .

And then it touched.

Instantly, the bubble burst with a short, sharp hiss and Tom dropped to the ground amid a tingly spattering of drizzle. He had landed close to the edge of the runway so that if anyone appeared at the gate he could quickly hide in the surrounding undergrowth. He straightened up and was surprised to discover that his legs felt heavy. Then he reminded himself that he'd spent most of the day inside the bubble floating weightlessly, like an astronaut on a space walk. It was bound to take him a while to get his earth-legs back. He walked towards the gate in a slow, crouching motion, stopping every so often to rest and listen. All was silent except for the faint rustling of the bamboo canes either side of the runway. He was close enough now to the gate to see the sign posted just inside it.

'BEWARE,' it said. 'Low-flying golf balls.' Very funny, thought Tom, edging closer to read the line of smaller type printed in brackets underneath. He didn't find that quite so amusing. '(And alligators)', it said. Suddenly the rustling among the bamboo canes sounded altogether more sinister. He ran to the middle of the runway and scanned the undergrowth on either side. Nothing. Perhaps it was just a joke.

His body still felt heavy, so he decided that the most sensible thing to do would be to walk quietly and calmly towards the gate, running only if he spotted an alligator about to join him on the tarmac. But already it was too late. As he looked back towards the gate he found his path blocked. A large alligator, sporting three curious lumps on its head each the size of a boiled egg, was ambling towards him up the centre of the runway, its eyes glowing red in the moonlight. Tom didn't move.

He knew he couldn't outrun it – his legs were still leaden. Neither did he dare move off the runway into the swampland in case he came face to face with Three Lumps' relatives. He would have to defend himself. But how? All he had with him was the rope he'd taken from the frogman, coiled up over his shoulder. Perhaps he could lasso it. Using a lasso to catch cattle was the one skill he'd taken from Hopper. And wasn't that how they caught alligators – by lassoing their snouts and pulling the rope tight? But he could only lasso one alligator at a time, and already another had left the comfort of its swamp in search of an easy meal. As they sauntered lazily towards him Tom looked behind him for a way of escape, only to find, to his heart-pounding horror, that two more were closing in from the opposite direction, swinging their heavily armoured tails behind them. He was trapped. No wonder they were all grinning.

He wanted to cry for help. From his father. From anyone. Even from Mr Kruud. But he didn't dare. He was sure that as soon as he made a noise the alligators would rush at him. Besides, he was beyond rescue now. Already they were so close that he could hear their claws scratching against the tarmac as they walked. Suddenly, he remembered the bottle of concentrated 3F, the Fizzle Flying Formula which he'd stuffed into his back pocket before escaping from Kruud's ship. It was his only hope. The alligators were advancing towards him on three sides, forcing him closer and closer to the swamp. He pulled out the bottle and backed slowly to the side of the runway. He looked over his shoulder. A patch of stinking swamp water lay a few feet beyond. It was fringed with tall bamboo canes, but there was a gap just wide enough for Tom to reach the water safely. Suddenly he turned and ran to the edge. He emptied half the bottle of 3F concentrate into the swamp, then took the rope from his shoulder and uncoiled it. The weight and feel of it in his hands seemed strangely familiar, as though he'd worked with ropes all his life. Intuitively, he tied a loop in one end with a slip knot and threw it into the water, quickly twirling it around so that the Fizzle Flying Formula soaked deep into the rope's fibres. Then he pulled it out, heavy and dripping, and jumped back on to the runway, midway between the alligators approaching him. He could see the thin skin of Fizzle inside the hoop. But would it work? Seymour hadn't tested the formula in ordinary water yet, let alone swamp water.

Holding the other end tightly in his left hand he began spinning the loop above his head with his right arm, swivelling his wrist as though he were stirring an upside-down cup of tea. The faster it spun the bigger the loop grew. Tom didn't take his eyes off the advancing alligators for a second. As soon as the loop was wide enough he would let it fall over him. At the same time he would jump upwards, launching himself through the shimmering Fizzle skin to escape in a new bubble. At least, that was his plan. And it might have worked too, had not Three Lumps chosen that moment to charge at him. Instinctively, Tom lowered the loop in front of him in a feeble attempt to create a protective barrier between them. Of course, it was too flimsy to resist half a ton of ravenous alligator. Three Lumps lunged through the hoop, its powerful, gaping jaws ready to take a deadly grip of Tom's legs.

'Aaaargh!' Tom screamed and stumbled backwards, tripping over his feet and falling flat on to the tarmac. He looked up quickly. But then, instead of jumping to his feet, he threw himself back down again and lay still. Tensing every muscle in an effort to press himself deep into the tarmac he watched, wide-eyed, as the soft, pale underbelly of the alligator, now an unwilling passenger in a murky but perfectly formed Fizzle bubble, glided slowly and serenely over him. As the bubble floated just inches above his body towards his face, he held his breath and pressed his cheek flat against the runway. He knew that should his nose or anything else touch the bubble it would burst, and the alligator would fall on top of him. He was paralysed. Pinned to the ground, all he could do was watch as the other alligators continued to lumber towards him. And wait. Finally the bubble passed, moving so closely over his cheek that his skin tingled, before heading into the swampy darkness.

As soon as it was clear Tom leaped up and snatched the rope from the tarmac. To his relief a thin, quivering film remained inside the loop, having been replenished instantly from the Fizzle Formula stored in the saturated rope fibres. How many bubbles the loop could produce before the rope dried out Tom didn't know, but two more of the alligators were almost on him, staring hungrily at his legs. Frantically, he began to spin the loop in front of him as fast as he could, simultaneously feeding the rope through his hands to push it further and further away from him. And not a moment too soon. As the alligators lunged at him one after the other, two more bubbles skimmed over the ground towards him, pushing him towards a clump of bamboo at the edge of the runway. As he felt the edge of the tarmac through the sole of his shoe he looked behind him. The bamboo canes were moving. He didn't dare step any closer to them for fear of what might be waiting there to greet him. The bubbles were either side of him now, and moving closer together. He turned himself sideways to make himself as thin as possible, hoping to edge between the two and return to the relative safety of the middle of the runway. But the gap was too narrow. He was sandwiched in between the two, unable to move forwards, backwards or sideways. Slowly the two alligators turned their heads towards him, and the bubbles rotated accordingly. Tom found himself staring into the teeth of the alligator in front of him whilst, behind him, the second alligator's flared nostrils were so close to the back of his head that he could hear it breathing. Now the bubbles were edging closer together, blocking Tom's only escape route and forcing him back, inch by inch, towards the swamp. He was trapped. He had to make a choice, and quickly. Either he could wait until the bubbles touched him, or indeed each other, sending both alligators tumbling to his feet. Or, he could retreat into the swamp and take his chances there. He couldn't decide. Instead, he froze, staring transfixed into the eyes of the alligator whose snout was now just inches away from his face, and drifting closer. It was too late to do anything. The bubble was about to touch his nose. At the same time, sensing that supper was about to be served, the alligator opened its huge slavering mouth.

Immediately, as its top jaw lifted upwards so the bubble rose a foot higher in response. Tom took his chance. He threw himself flat on the ground and, with his arms pressed tightly against his sides, rolled over and over underneath the bubble until he reached the other side. Then he leaped back on to his feet and sprinted to the centre of the runway, glancing back just in time to see the second alligator raise its head to watch the first, and itself begin to rise, before drifting out over the swampland.

Now, only one alligator remained between Tom and the gate. He checked that another film of Fizzle Flying Formula had formed inside the loop, then advanced towards it. He didn't want to lose the rope – it might yet help him escape. If he could tempt the last alligator to jump through the loop he might at last make it to the gate. Tom's heart was pounding. All he had to do was keep the loop spinning and wait for the alligator to jump through. He'd managed it three times already. Once more and he would be home and dry. Suddenly there was a loud splash behind him. One of the bubbles had touched the top of a bamboo cane and burst, sending Three Lumps crashing back into the swamp. Then there was another crash. Then another. Huge, towering sprays of foul-smelling swamp water rose into the air and fell like rain on to the runway. Tom ducked as the water landed on him, soaking his shirt and momentarily breaking his rhythm. The loop faltered and lost its shape, just as the alligator lunged at him.

A large yellow fang protruding from its lower jaw snagged the rope on its way through, pulling the loop further out of shape so that one of its front legs also became ensnared. As the leg folded under it and the alligator stumbled to a halt a few feet in front of him, Tom tugged the rope hard, closing the loop to pull the jaw and leg tightly together. Then, with a few expert flicks of his wrist he sent several open loops rolling down the rope like a series of waves. As they broke over the alligator's drooling snout he tugged them tight, and for a few seconds the animal, bemused that its jaws had suddenly locked shut just when it was thinking of using them, became so entangled that it couldn't move without toppling over. It was all the time Tom needed. His legs no longer felt heavy. As more hungry predators began to appear on the runway behind him he sprinted past the alligator and leaped on to the gates, clawing his way to the top before throwing himself down on to the dirt track on the other side. His legs buckled under him and he collapsed on to his back in a cloud of dust. But at last he was safe. Panting heavily, he stared up at the full moon, and allowed himself a smile. Low-flying alligators, he thought, remembering the sign by the gate. Ha! If only Mr Kruud knew. Relieved and exhausted, he closed his eyes.

When he reopened them moments later the moon had gone, eclipsed by the two shadowy faces staring down at him.

Into the Volcano

'Get up, hurry! Bamboo-masters are coming.'

Pepe and Paco pulled Tom to his feet and dragged him to the side of the track, just as the bright headlights of an alligator-proof golf buggy lit up the gate. Crouching low, they bundled him along the front row of oil drums.

'Fifth drum along,' Pepe told him. 'Get in quick – they're almost here.'

Despite their filthy, rag-tag appearance Tom felt instantly that he could trust the boys, so he dived head-first into the empty drum and curled himself up into a tight ball at the bottom. To his surprise Pepe landed on top of him a second later, and clamped a small but firm hand over his mouth.

'Shhh . . .' he whispered. 'Don't make a sound.'

Tom could tell from the fingernails digging deep into his arm that Pepe was scared, too, so he kept still and silent, ignoring the pain and the sound of his own heartbeat in order to hear what was happening outside. At first, all he heard was the low humming of the golf buggy's motor. But when it reached the oil drums another sound joined it as the driver reached out, laughing, and dragged his bamboo cane along them like a burst of machine-gun fire – rat-a-tat-a-tat-a-tat-a-tat-a-tat-a-tat. When the cane struck Pepe's oil drum Tom's whole body jumped to avoid the bullet which he thought had been fired into it. As his head crashed against the inside of the drum with a dull, painful clang, Pepe tightened his grip over Tom's mouth in case he cried out. But already it was too late. The humming had stopped, and been replaced by the soft, dusty shuffle of footsteps. Tom couldn't tell which way they were heading, only that they were very close. Then they too came to a halt. Tom held his breath, tucking his hands and feet tight into his body in one last desperate attempt to avoid the long, grabbing arms which he knew were about to reach in and seize him. But instead he felt Pepe's grip loosen as he recognised the reassuring rattle of the gates being opened, then closed again once the buggy had passed through on to the runway. Pepe peered through one of the small spy holes punched around the side of the drum.

'They've gone,' he confirmed, just as Paco climbed in to join them.

After much shuffling about the three boys squatted to face each other in a cramped, knee-bumping huddle.

'Thank you,' said Tom, finally. 'I'm sure they'd have caught me if you hadn't come along. What are you doing out here?'

'We live here,' Pepe explained.

'You mean in the huts at the back?' asked Tom.

'No! Those are for bamboo-masters only,' said Pepe. 'We live here, in these oil drums. This one's mine, and Paco's just moved in next door.'

Tom frowned. Surely no one could live in an oil drum, could they?

'But . . . what do you do when it rains?' he asked.

Pepe and Paco looked puzzled. Didn't this boy know anything?

'We turn them upside down, of course,' Paco replied.

Still Tom couldn't quite believe it.

'But . . . aren't you scared living alone out here?'

The two boys burst out laughing.

'What's so funny?' asked Tom.

'Look outside,' said Paco.

Slowly Tom raised himself up and peered over the rim of the oil drum. The track lay in front of him and, beyond that, nothing but rough ground, sloping upwards from right to left as it merged with the base of the volcano. Bemused, he turned around, just in time to glimpse a thousand grimy faces duck back into their steel sleeping quarters.

'They won't come out,' Pepe explained, pulling Tom down. 'We've been ordered to stay in our drums until Mr Kruud's visitors have gone.'

'I'm glad you didn't,' observed Tom.

'We couldn't, not after we heard you call for help,' Paco explained.

'But I didn't make a sound,' Tom replied.

Pepe hesitated.

'Well . . . I suppose it was more of a feeling really,' he conceded. 'Somehow we both knew you were out there and needed our help.'

Their words reminded Tom of the moment he finally 'Got the Fizzle', just as that horrible woman from the Council was pushing Polly beneath the surface of the Shipley Manor moat. Instantly he'd felt Polly's fear as though it were his own, and known that he had to save her.

'I don't suppose you've tasted any special . . . fizzy water lately, have you?' he asked them.

'Yes!' they both cried. 'Mr Kruud and the fish woman made us drink it.'

'Fish woman?' Tom asked, imagining the cheerful,

rather plump lady who ran the fish stall at Shipley market.

'We don't know her real name,' Pepe told him, 'but she smells like the fish guts we're made to eat whenever we do something really bad, like stick a Kola label on crooked.'

'She's as thin as a bamboo-master's cane, too,' Paco added. 'When she stands next to Mr Kruud they look like a big number 10.'

Tom smiled, then listened intently as the boys told him everything they knew about the bottling factory, and the bamboo-masters, and their boss Sherman H. Kruud. But nothing they said explained why such a cruel and greedy man as he would be so interested in the Fizzle, let alone why it appeared to trust him. As for Polly's strange behaviour, that was as big a mystery as ever. When they'd finished talking Tom felt as though he'd been handed a few pieces of jigsaw but still had no idea what the final picture was supposed to look like. But he was certain of one thing. If the Captain knew about Pepe and Paco and the rest of the children being forced to live outside in those filthy oil drums he'd want nothing to do with Mr Kruud. He had to tell him as soon as possible.

'Can you show me a way into the cave?' he asked.

Pepe and Paco glanced at each other. They knew

that soon the bamboo-masters would be inspecting the oil drums to check that everyone was obeying Kruud's orders, and that anyone caught defying them would be made to 'walk the runway'. But they knew also that they had to help Tom. For some reason connected to the fizzy water this strange fair-haired boy felt like a brother to them.

'We can take you as far as the factory,' Pepe offered, 'but after that we'll have to get back in time for drum inspection. And we'll have to hurry.'

That suited Tom fine.

'I'm ready,' he said.

The two small boys climbed out and led Tom along the front row of oil drums adjoining the track. Every few seconds, as they crouched briefly behind one of the drums to listen for any approaching golf buggies, Tom would catch curious, beady eyes staring at him through the spy holes in their sides, only for them to disappear the instant he returned their gaze. Once the oil drums were behind them they quickened their pace along the straight, gently rising track, darting between the scattering of loose rocks and bushes which littered the dusty ground on either side. When it met the base of the volcano the ground rose steeply, and the track veered right to begin its long snaking climb to the top. After ten minutes the three boys reached the first bend and rested against a large rock whose tumbling descent down the mountainside had ended abruptly at the side of the track. Tom estimated that they were now almost level with the top of the cave mouth, yet so far he'd seen no sign of a way in.

'We have to go up higher,' Pepe explained. 'There's no direct way into the cave from here. You'll have to go into the factory which is on the floor above it, then find your way down from there. Come on.'

They continued along the track to the second bend, where Pepe and Paco stopped in front of a pair of double doors. These had been painted in a collection of mottled greys and browns to match the surrounding rock – presumably, Tom thought, to go unnoticed by any passing aircraft or cargo ships.

'You'll be able to find your way from here,' Pepe told him. 'Just make sure the bamboo-masters don't catch you.'

'Especially Moolah,' Paco added over his shoulder as he joined his friend running back down the slope.

Tom watched the two boys disappear into the darkness. Then, slowly, he opened one of the doors . . . and stepped inside.

The wide corridor stretched away in both directions, its bare concrete floor and whitewashed walls curving gently away from him as it circled the bottling factory. Several large open doorways were set into the inner wall, from which filthy strips of plastic hung limply, allowing buggies, fork-lift trucks and other vehicles to move freely in and out.

He turned through the first doorway, almost walking into the path of a bamboo-master. Ducking in between two huge stacks of bottles, Tom waited until he'd passed, then peered out. The factory floor was swarming with them. Patrolling, no doubt under instructions that on no account should he get close to the Captain and the others. He looked around. Almost too late he saw three bamboo-masters keeping watch from the viewing platform high to his right. To his left, rising up amid the towers of bottle crates were the four huge storage tanks. Tom had kept his bearings and knew that the cave entrance was to his left. Perhaps those four tanks were directly above the Fizzle in the cave below. Then he spotted his shipmates. They were mere specks directly in front of him on the far side of the factory, as far away as spectators at the opposite end of a football ground, but Slugbucket's height, the Captain's beard and Seymour's wheelchair were all unmistakable. They were moving around like a group of tourists behind a guide who, dressed in white and wearing a large stetson hat, could only have been one person. Tom looked around him. If he was to warn the Captain about Kruud he would have to get closer. So, darting between stacks of bottles, crouching low alongside the conveyor belts, he began slowly to weave his way towards them. But the closer he got the more bamboo-masters he encountered in his path, until he realised that a ring of them had been placed around his shipmates, preventing him from reaching them.

He crouched down behind a huge stack of boxes. To his surprise and further confusion he saw that they appeared to contain Fizzle labels. Surely he couldn't be wrong about Kruud, could he? As he looked more closely he noticed that the corner of a label stuck on the outside of one of the boxes had curled up. He peeled it back to reveal the Kruud Kola label underneath. He dug his fingernail into the cardboard and ripped the box open, revealing the huge slab of labels inside. He took a handful. Kruud Kola, Kruud Kola, Kruud Kola. There were no Fizzle labels. This was just another trick to fool the Captain, and judging by the way his shipmates were following Kruud around on their factory tour it seemed to be working. He stuffed a couple of the labels into his pocket and tried to move closer, but he could find no way past the bamboo-masters. He looked up to see the giant mechanical grabbers motionless, as if asleep, their legs folded neatly together. If only he could hitch a ride on one, or use it to drop a box of fake labels at the Captain's feet. If the box burst open to reveal their true contents, maybe at last the Captain would realise that Kruud was as fake as those labels. But he had no idea how the grabbers were controlled. He would have to find another way. He would try to contact Polly again. He'd tried before but she hadn't responded, almost as if she were asleep or unconscious. But seeing her skip along behind Slugbucket it was clear that she was once again very much awake.

He closed his eyes and began counting backwards. Finally, he succeeded, suddenly feeling Polly's presence.

'Polly, it's me – Tom. Don't look behind you.'

Throughout Polly's life the Captain had reminded her that, like umbrellas, minds only worked properly when they were open. So, unlike Tom, Polly had *always* believed that anything was possible, welcoming into her mind every strange thought and fantastic idea that crossed her path, so that even though she was just ten years old it had become a rich and exciting place. When Pike first tried to enter Polly's mind she had searched long and hard for the entrance, before realising that there wasn't one. Instead, it was laid out like a huge open-air market set in the middle of the English countryside, with no doors or walls to keep ideas in or out, and no roof to stop them from taking off. With hundreds of colourful stalls buckling under the weight of everything from fabrics and fireworks to curries and Fizzle cocktails, and yet more displaying Polly's hopes and dreams, fears and regrets for all to see, the market thronged with life. Fizzlefish and silver seahorses swam through the bubble-filled air, whilst Polly's numerous costumes strolled around by themselves, browsing the stalls and chatting idly about the day's goings-on with the sheep and other creatures from the Shipley Manor Estate.

Among them walked Pike, unseen amid the bustle, listening carefully to these country gossips as they discussed everything that Polly was hearing, and seeing, and feeling. Once she realised that these conversations were, in fact, Polly's thoughts, planting new ones in her mind – even persuading Polly that pink was her new favourite colour – had proved to be easy. All she had to do was . . . start a rumour.

'The Fizzle ssssays,' she would tell a passing palm tree, 'that Jamaica is the *only* place to be this time of year.' Then she would watch and listen as the rumour spread, growing louder and louder with every passing second until the sound of it filled the air, and fireworks announced it in exploding pink letters across the sky. Each time the Fizzle spoke to Polly in this way the sound quickly filled her head, leaving no room for doubt. The Fizzle was always right. The Fizzle would always protect her. The Fizzle had always to be obeyed. And the Fizzle . . . was that voice.

Now, as Tom began to tell Polly about the oil drums and fake Fizzle labels, Venetia Pike bent down to deliver a message into the ear of a grazing sheep.

'Did you know, ssssweetie,' she whispered, 'that Tom is a traitor?' So that, within a few seconds, Polly could no longer hear what Tom was telling her. Instead, her head pounded to the sound of Pike's words being endlessly repeated, hissed, howled, clucked, buzzed, barked, bleated and brayed, by every creature, real and imaginary, that lived inside her mind:

'Tom is a traitor. Tom is a traitor. Tom is a trai-ai-ai-ai-t-or-or-or!'

She leaned back against a bottling machine, clutching her head. Now she knew. Tom didn't want the world to 'Get the Fizzle' at all. He was trying to sabotage their hard work and ruin everything. She turned away from her companions and glared accusingly at him. Then, as he stared back in disbelief, she raised her arm and pointed at him.

'There's Tom,' she announced, loudly. 'Sssstop him!'

At once the Captain turned, his face broadening into a huge smile of relief.

'Ahoy there, shipmate,' he called out. 'We've been worri . . .'

But already Tom had gone. Too far away to be heard and with his route to the Captain blocked, he had started to run, pursued by Moolah and the other bamboo-masters.

'What in the Seven Seas is wrong with the poor boy?' the Captain muttered as he and Kruud and the rest of the Shipley Manor crew followed them. But at least, he told himself, he was safe.

Tom knew otherwise, of course. He didn't know what the bamboo-masters would do when they caught him, but they weren't about to reunite him with his shipmates, he was sure of that. He ran towards the far end of the factory, glancing back to find that one of his pursuers, keys jangling wildly on her belt, had kicked off her flip-flops and was catching up with him fast.

At the same time, from their lookout positions on the viewing platform, Luka and the two other bamboo-masters had reached for their remote controls and brought a trio of metallic spiders to life. They sent the grabbers speeding across the ceiling after Tom, their cog wheels whining along the cables and flicking up sparks, which showered down like hot rain as they accelerated. They soon gained ground on Tom, and by the time he reached the storage tanks one of them had already overtaken Moolah and begun slowly to lower itself above him. As he raced back into open space, two rows of bottle-stacks loomed up in front of him like an avenue of skyscrapers. In the wall at the far end of this bottle boulevard Tom spotted a door. At last, some hope of escape. He sprinted towards the front two stacks, oblivious to the giant metallic legs opening just inches above his head. They began to lower themselves around him and for an instant one of the legs appeared in front of his nose. Then just as suddenly, it was gone. As he ran between the twin stacks it had tried to follow him. But with its huge metallic legs splayed out ready to take Tom in its grip, the spider was too wide to continue the chase and had collided with both stacks with a deafening crash, slamming into the bottles about halfway up. Tom ducked and kept running as the bottles exploded into a million flying fragments and fell like jagged hailstones behind him. Then, one after another, the stacks either side of him began to tumble over, as the first stack tipped over on to the next, which fell on to the next, which smashed into the next. Glass filled the air as bottles rained down, spinning out of their crates and crashing on to the hard concrete floor like a thousand falling chandeliers. As the stacks fell Tom kept running, pursued now only by Moolah, her bare heels in hot pursuit just inches ahead of the blizzard of broken glass that threatened any moment to catch and engulf them. Tom reached the door a heartbeat ahead of her. He tore through it on to a metal staircase which zigzagged downwards, hurling himself down the steps two at a time before jumping the last four and bursting through the door at the bottom, on to the jetty. And then the bamboo-master was in the doorway. Tom turned and backed, panting, towards the water as Moolah locked the door behind her and stood facing him. Shipley Manor was moored a short distance to Tom's right, its drawbridge inviting him to run on board and hide until the Captain returned. Beyond that was the cave mouth, through which Fizzle was being sucked greedily towards the five pipes at the rear of the cave.

Moolah anticipated what Tom would do next,

and as he made a dash for the drawbridge she moved swiftly to block his way and force him back to the far end of the jetty. When he reached the last plank he stopped, and Moolah drew the bamboo cane slowly out of her belt. Tom looked down into the fast-flowing water behind him, then up at the control lever set into the rock to his left. Perhaps if he could turn off the pumps he might have enough time to swim to the cave mouth and escape under the security grille. He had no other choice. He lunged for the lever and attempted to push it back up, only to find that it was locked in position. Then, as Moolah flew at him he stepped back into thin air and tumbled sideways into the water. Instantly the current took hold of him and swept him backwards towards the pipes. Even a good swimmer like his mother would have been carried away, so Tom, who had learned to swim only recently, had no chance. Moolah slid the cane back into her belt and watched silently as Tom, his arms and legs flailing wildly against the current, was carried past the first pipe, then the second, then the third, then the fourth, before finally disappearing feet first, like a dead fly up a vacuum cleaner, into the fifth.

Tom's Discovery

Tom shot upwards inside the pipe towards the cave roof, his feet leading the way in a perfect reverse dive, his eyes closed in the desperate hope that he might yet wake up to find himself back home in Shipley. But the roar of water around him wouldn't let him forget where he was. He noticed the sound become more muffled as the pipe travelled through solid rock, then change back again as it emerged inside the bottling factory and continued past the storage tanks on its way to the next level. Seconds later, Tom was fired like a torpedo into dark, open water, drawing a long trail of silvery bubbles behind him. As he slowed down, other currents began to tumble him around in the darkness until he had no idea which way was up, and which was down. Already his lungs were burning as though they were about to explode. And yet there was no sign of the Fizzle rescuing him – no cool, life-giving gas bubble forming around his head to escort him safely to the surface. Instead, all he could feel was the last pocket of air escaping from the side of his mouth. As it brushed across his cheek on its way to the surface, he kicked out to follow it. Once, twice, three times. But it was too late. Suddenly, an irresistible urge to open his mouth erupted out of his lungs and tore like hot lava into his throat. Reaching up to feel nothing but water between his outstretched fingers, one last thought filled his head: Why hasn't the Fizzle saved me?

And then he broke the surface.

Air flooded into his lungs in long, urgent gasps. He tipped his head back, greedily sucking in all that he could, his eyes closed to savour each delicious mouthful. When, at last, he opened them he saw that he was underneath some kind of flat roof, or lid, which appeared to be suspended a few metres above his head. He turned himself around and discovered that he was floating in the centre of a vast circular tank about the width of a football pitch. Slowly he began to swim towards the bright halo of light which marked the gap between the roof and the rim of the tank. Eventually, as he neared the side he could see that the water was still several feet below the rim, inching its way up. But he couldn't wait for it to rise to make his escape. Soon every drop of Fizzle would have been sucked into the tank and be lost to them. He had to find a way out quickly. He swam around the edge until he spotted two pieces of metal protruding above the rim on the outside of the tank. They looked as though they might belong to the top of a ladder which, if he could somehow reach it, might also lead him down to the ground. He thought for a moment, then allowed himself to sink below the surface while he unbuckled and pulled out his belt. Then he pushed back to the surface and, pedalling hard to stay afloat, pushed the end of the belt through the buckle until he'd made a small loop at the end. Hardly wide enough to lasso an alligator, he thought, but perhaps he could hook it over the top of the ladder. Using one hand to stay afloat, he swung the belt overhead with the other, then launched it upwards towards the rim. It missed the ladder and fell back into the water. So he tried again, and again, until, finally, he managed to hook the loop over the top of the ladder. Then, gripping the belt with both hands, he started to walk up the inside of the tank until he was able to grab the rim and heave himself over the edge, on to the ladder.

Nervously, he watched the Fizzle rain down from his soaking-wet clothes to spatter noisily on the ground a hundred feet below. Luckily, no one appeared to be there to hear it, so he began to climb down. Then he stopped. The tank reminded him of something. Tall and cylindrical with a flat lid – it reminded him of the glass Fizzle Filter that Seymour had used to feed Fizzle gas to the two slugs. The roof was only a metre above the end of the ladder. Perhaps he could take a look on top. He climbed back up and, with one hand still on the ladder, reached up to grasp the edge. Then he pulled himself upright and peered over. The roof was flat and, as far as Tom could tell from tapping it with his knuckles, made of solid metal. In the centre sat a clear glass dome about the same size and shape as an igloo. Tom was too far away to see what was inside it, but he had to find out. Carefully he stepped on to the top rung of the ladder, then levered himself up and rolled on to the roof. Then, having crawled safely away from the edge, he stood up and began squelching towards the dome. Upon reaching it he saw that a glass door was set flush into its side, with a small gold key protruding from the lock. He turned the key and the door popped open, sighing gently as its airtight seal was broken and warm air rushed out across Tom's face. He stepped inside.

The centre of the dome was dominated by a solid metal rod, like a fireman's pole, which extended up from the floor, passing through the glass towards the roof of the chamber. There it was attached to the biggest motor Tom had ever seen. He could see only one possible use for the rod: to push the lid down. A studded metal walkway stretched around the inside of the dome, from which four more led into the centre, dividing the circle into quarters. The metal rod was attached firmly to the floor in the middle where they met. In the areas between the walkways the floor appeared to be made from a duller, softer material. Tom knelt down and ran his fingertips over the surface to discover that it was made from a fine wire mesh. He took off one of his waterlogged shoes, which somehow had survived the journey, and tipped the Fizzle out of it. As he suspected, the water refused to filter through, instead forming a small puddle on the surface. Next he knelt down, pressed his lips up against the mesh and blew. Again, as he expected, his breath passed through instantly. There was no doubt about it. He was standing on top of an enormous Fizzle Filter. But why? The answer was staring him in the face. Around the walkway, bolted to the floor at each of the junctions as though they were marking the points of a compass, were four leather chairs. Three black. One white. Tom walked from chair to chair, reading the names engraved on small metal plates attached to the back of each one. Ching, Punjabootee, Robovich and finally . . . Kruud.

So that was it. The world wasn't going to 'Get the Fizzle' at all. Kruud and the others wanted it for one reason only. To breathe in the gas and obtain the same powers as himself and Polly and Hopper. Had Pike been there she would have been equally horrified. After all, these were the same three billionaires who she and Kruud had agreed to blackmail. But Tom knew nothing about that. Or about Pike. All he knew was that Kruud and his friends had to be stopped. He ran back to the edge of the tank and lowered himself carefully on to the ladder. Then he began the long climb down. As he stepped on to the floor of the chamber, Moolah was waiting for him. She leaped out from nowhere, pushing him to the ground, pinning his arms behind his back and pressing his cheek hard against the concrete. A pair of white, diamond-buckled shoes approached, escorted by several pairs of flip-flops. They stopped in front of Tom's nose.

'Howdy,' said the white shoes. 'Glad you could drop in. Let him up.'

Moolah took her knee out of Tom's back and he climbed on to his feet. Kruud smiled.

'You know, you're the only one of your friends who's got any brains. Why don't you work for me?

I'm about to become leader of the richest, most exclusive, most rootin' tootin' club in the world.'

'What's the point of being rich?' replied Tom, shivering. 'There's always someone richer than you.'

'Not if your name's Sherman H. Kruud there ain't, boy. Not any more. You're looking at the new Number One.'

Tom seemed unimpressed. Kruud continued anyway, enjoying his moment of triumph.

'You see, I kinda liked your idea of sharin' the Fizzle. So I got ma boys at the Kruud Oil an' Gas Corporation to build me this little gas extractor tank so I could share it with ma three new business buddies. For a price, of course. Half their businesses in return for one of the hottest seats on the planet. An' you know what, they were happy to pay. So, instead of makin' three powerful enemies I got myself three powerful allies. An' believe me, we *will* be powerful. Once we've guzzled that fine Fizzle gas down into our lungs we'll have the greatest weapon ever seen on the boardroom battlefield.'

He took a bottle of Fizzle from his jacket and swung it in front of Tom's face.

'Yes sirree! With a bottle of this in every meeting we'll know what our opponents are thinking, we'll be able to out-bluff them, outmanoeuvre them, out-negotiate them. We'll be invincible.'

He stepped closer.

'We're gonna share our skills, too. If my hunch is right, by this time tomorrow I'll be able to count my money in seven languages, pilot a submarine and play a tune on the balalaika. I may even,' he added, prodding his forefinger menacingly against Tom's forehead, 'pay your mind a visit to see what puny little skills it has to offer.'

Tom swallowed hard.

'But . . . why do you want to be even richer?'

Kruud glared at him, impatiently. Clearly the boy was an idiot, after all. He pulled a meringue from his pocket and held it up in the palm of his hand.

'Did you ever dip a sponge into the bath, boy, till it was so full of water it was heavy in your hands?'

Tom nodded.

'Then whaddya do? You squeezed it, didn't you, boy? But you didn't stop halfway. No sirrreee. You squeezed every last itty-bitty drop of water outta that sponge till it was light as a feather, ain't that right? And do you know why? Because you *could*, that's why. Because it's "human nature". An' that's all I'm doin'. The world is just one giant sponge drippin' with people and money, and I'm gonna keep squeezin' till it's as dry as this here meringue. An' let me tell you, boy, no one – least of all a bunch of save-the-world do-gooders – is gonna stop me.'

Kruud closed his fist tight around the meringue and it exploded in a shower of crumbs. He licked the sticky remnants off his fingers. 'Mmmm, not bad.'

'But that's not fair on everyone else!' Tom protested.

'Fair? *Fair*?' Kruud replied angrily. 'Fairness is for the fairies, boy, and I sure as hell don't believe in those, no more than I believe in right an' wrong, an' good an' bad. There's only winnin' and losin', an' I make damn sure I win every time. Here . . . catch.'

Kruud sent a silver dollar spinning through the air towards Tom.

'Heads,' he called out just as Tom caught it.

Tom opened his hand. Sure enough it was heads. He turned the coin over. Heads again.

'See what I mean? Now lock this loser up, Molly, while I decide what to do with him.'

'Moolah,' the bamboo-master reminded him quietly. 'My name's Moolah.'

Kruud stepped up to her, crimson-faced.

'I don't care two cents what your name is, girl,' he yelled, spraying meringue crumbs in her face. 'Just do as I say!'

Then he stomped out of the chamber, pausing only to bark one last order from the exit.

'An' make sure I get that damn coin back!'

Moolah barred Tom's way while Luka rustled up

a padlock and chain from a nearby locker. Then Moolah stepped forward and held out her hand. Tom dropped the coin into it and for a brief moment, as their eyes met, he smiled. Instantly, the bamboo-master delivered a hard, stinging slap across his face.

'Don't you *dare* feel sorry for me,' she spat.

But Tom *was* sorry. The world was full of people who cared what *he* was called – his father, his grandparents, his aunties, uncles and cousins, his friends at school and, of course, the Captain and all his Shipley Manor crewmates. He could only imagine how lonely he would feel if they didn't.

The two bamboo-masters chained Tom to a pipe on the wall and left. On the way out Moolah tossed the coin to Luka.

'You can take it back to him,' she said.

A few minutes later Moolah slammed the door of her tin hut behind her and threw herself face down on to her bunk. Then she heard a familiar sound. She turned over to watch a lone white moth dancing clumsily around the bare light bulb overhead, casting a shadow ten times its real size on to the ceiling. She had worked in Kruud's factory from the age of five, and had grown up to become his most loyal and ruthless bamboo-master. Every child on the island feared and hated her, whilst the other bamboo-masters resented her because she was so much faster and tougher and smarter than they were and, to make matters worse, a girl. But she had always hoped that Kruud might feel something for her, if not affection then at least some spark of recognition for all her hard work. Instead, he constantly disappointed her and, today, he couldn't even remember her name. Worse still, he didn't care. She was alone like that stupid little moth, flying slavishly around something that neither knew nor cared that she existed. But she didn't want to feel that way. She rolled back on to her tummy and slipped her hand under the pillow.

Good – it was still there.

Slugbucket's Slippery Snack

Tom's shipmates had searched every inch of the house and apart from Slugbucket, who was still checking the roof, had gathered back in the kitchen. They had all seen Tom disappear through the doorway leading down to the cave, but by the time they had climbed over the mountain of broken glass blocking their way and reached the jetty, he was nowhere to be found. Even his fastest bamboo-master, Kruud informed them after Moolah had whispered in his ear, hadn't been quick enough to catch the poor boy. So, either he had swum under the security grille and out of the cave, which was highly unlikely given the speed of the current, or he was hiding somewhere inside Shipley Manor. Then Kruud had left, assuring the

Captain that he would organise a search outside whilst he and his crew searched the house. And, in the meantime, Operation 'Get the Fizzle' would continue.

That had been an hour ago, and despite their doing everything except take up the floorboards, Tom hadn't turned up.

The Captain was pacing up and down, poking and prodding his beard as though Tom might be hiding inside it.

'There's something starting to smell very fishy about this,' he was saying. 'Tom's the most sensible boy I've ever met. Why has he been behaving like this? There has to be a reason.'

'I've got it,' Seymour cried out, suddenly.

'You mean you know why Tom's been behaving so oddly?' the Captain asked him.

'No,' Seymour replied, 'I've worked out what was odd about the factory. There were no workers in it.'

'We could all see that, old chap,' the Captain replied, 'but surely that's because it's fully automatic like Mr Kruud told us. The machines do everything.'

'I know that's what he said,' replied Seymour, 'but did you see any labelling machines, or ones to put the bottle tops on, or pack the bottles into boxes ready for distribution?'

No one spoke.

'Exactly! That's because there weren't any. Mr Kruud has *lied* to us. And that's not all,' he continued. 'Do you remember those four huge tanks which he told us were for storing the Fizzle before it was bottled?'

Everyone nodded.

'Well, don't you think it rather odd that there are five pipes sucking the Fizzle up from here, not four? Where does the other one go?'

'None of that proves anything,' said Polly.

'Oi think this does, though,' said Slugbucket, striding into the room. 'Oi didn't find any sign of Tom on the roof – I mean, top deck – but oi did find this floatin' in a puddle up there.'

He handed a damp newspaper clipping to the Captain. It was the same one Tom had seen pasted to the Crow's Nest window shortly before he jumped ship. The Captain read it carefully, his face hardening into a deep scowl.

'Blithering sea bass! I think this might be what Tom was trying to tell you about, Polly,' he said, handing her the piece of paper.

'It's a lie,' she said, barely looking at it. 'Tom's been tricked and now he's trying to trick us, too. Why would the Fizzle let anything bad happen?'

'I don't know,' said the Captain, pressing his teeth together, 'but I think it's time I asked Mr Kruud a few questions.'

He swept out of the room. Polly and the others followed him, then watched silently from the drawbridge as he rattled the door leading out of the cave. It was locked. Next he strode to the end of the jetty and grabbed the lever controlling the pipes, trying, as Tom had done an hour earlier, to turn off the pumps. The lever wouldn't budge. Finally, he walked, grim-faced, back to the drawbridge.

'Does any of you have something that will float?' he asked them.

'Oi do,' Slugbucket replied, taking a matchbox out of his pocket. He removed the slug from inside and handed over the empty box. The Captain tossed it straight into the water. The moment it hit the surface the Fizzle swept it towards the pipes. Then they watched the current carry the box past the first pipe, then the second, then the third, then the fourth before, finally, disappearing into the fifth.

'The other pipes must be fakes. That's the only one that's working,' the Captain observed, 'and I'd bet a pirate's pension it doesn't lead to any of those storage tanks.'

He hung his head. 'If anything's happened to

Tom I'll never forgive myself.'

'He's all roight,' said Slugbucket, whose face had become suddenly quite pale.

Polly turned to him.

'How do you know?' she asked, her own attempts at contacting Tom having given her another headache.

'Well . . . you know that slug oi took out the matchbox, one of them two that breathed in the Fizzle gas?'

'Yes.'

'Well . . . you said it was feelin' all cramped in there, didn't you, which means you was connected to it. An' I reckoned that Tom might be, too. So I thought it was worth a try, didn't I?'

'What was worth a try, Slugbucket?'

'I mean, it was an emergency. We got ter find young Tom some'ow, 'aven't we.'

'Slugbucket, what did you *do*?'

'I ate it,' he confessed, his mouth dropping down sadly at the corners. 'Poor thing. Tasted a bit loik mushroom. Anyway, the gas in its little lungs weren't much – just enough to connect me to Tom for 'alf a second or so – but I know where 'e is now. The answer sort o' popped into me 'ead.'

'So where is he?' asked the Captain.

'Up that poip,' Slugbucket said, pointing to the back of the cave.

Polly gasped.

'But 'e's all roight, I know he is,' Slugbucket added, shivering, ''cause I could feel it. He's cold an' wet an' exhausted, an' 'e ain't eaten since breakfast but 'e's still in one piece somewhere at the other end.'

The Captain turned to his crew.

'Well, shipmates, I for one have no idea what Mr Kruud is up to, but I have a sneaking suspicion that the Fizzle is being stolen from right under our noses. Do you think that's what Tom's been trying to tell you, Polly?'

But Polly wasn't listening. At least not to the Captain. Or even Tom. Instead, she was staring at the pipe. The Fizzle was talking to her again. Telling her to follow Tom and find out what was at the other end.

Suddenly there was a splash. The Captain turned to see Polly in the water, being carried towards the pipes as easily as the empty matchbox. Straightaway he jumped in after her as Maggie thrust Calypso on to Seymour's lap and raced to the end of the jetty. She hurled herself into the current just as Polly disappeared under the water. As the pipe sucked Polly into it Fizzlestick first, Maggie reached out in time to grab her ankle. Then the Captain joined her and together they tried to pull Polly out. But the flow was too strong.

Finally, the Captain began to prise Maggie's fingers away from her daughter.

'No, we can't let go, we can't!'

'We have to,' he shouted above the roar of the water. 'If we hold on to her any longer she'll drown.'

So they let the Fizzle take her. Maggie was still screaming for her daughter, fighting to follow her into the pipe, but the Captain knew it was too narrow for either of them. Instead, he held his hand out to Slugbucket, who had leant out over the edge of the jetty ready to pull them in. By the time Seymour returned from the house carrying a lifebelt the Captain and Maggie had climbed, dripping and exhausted, back on to the edge of the jetty.

For a moment the Captain remained there, glaring down at the Fizzle, his crimson face rigid with anger, his fists clenched at his side.

'What in the name of Neptune are you doing?' he screamed at it.

Finally through his rage he heard Maggie's cries as she beat her hands against the locked door.

'Let us out of here. *Let us out!*'

The Captain turned and put his hands gently on her shoulders.

'You need to stay and look after Calypso,' he said. 'The three of us will find the children, I promise.'

But she was having none of it.

'Seymour can look after Calypso,' she said. 'I'm going with you.'

'But . . .'

'I'm going!' she told him fiercely.

'Calypso will be fine with me, Captain,' Seymour assured him. 'I'll raise the drawbridge and let no one on board until you get back. Now go.'

Then he turned his wheelchair and, to Calypso's gurgling delight, bumpety-bumpety-bumped across the planks towards the house.

The Captain pulled Maggie gently away from the door.

'In that case you'd better stand clear,' he said. Then he nodded to Slugbucket, who had already dipped one of his massive shoulders ready to charge at the door. 'Ready when you are, shipmate.'

At the other end of the island, as Slugbucket was busy turning the cave door into a thousand flying splinters, Pike was also on the move. Intending to remain out of sight in Kruud's villa until every drop of Fizzle had been sucked into the four storage tanks, she had spent her time stretched out on one of his luxurious white leather sofas. Shrouded in silence, her pale, spidery hands crossed neatly over her chest and with no more than the occasional flickering of her closed eyelids to show that she was alive, she had wandered undisturbed through Polly's mind, listening to the gossips describe events as they unfolded in the bottling factory. When news spread of Tom's arrival she had delighted in persuading Polly to betray him. But he had escaped, and even though he hadn't been able to talk to his shipmates he had, somehow, managed to sow seeds of doubt in their minds. Only Polly's faith in the Fizzle remained unshakeable, growing stronger each time she heard Pike's voice, convinced that it was the voice of the Fizzle, the one voice that had to be obeyed. Around her, though, there was nothing but confusion and debate. Pike asked a passing sheep what was happening.

'The Captain thinks the Fizzle is wro-o-o-ong,' it bleated. 'He says To-o-o-om isn't a trai-ai-ai-t-or-or. Kru-u-u-ud is.'

'But the Fizzle is never wrong,' Pike reminded it, knowing her words would spread instantly to settle the matter.

'I kno-o-o-ow,' it replied, 'but that still doesn't expla-a-a-ain . . .' It paused to rip up a mouthful of grass. '. . . why only the fifth pi-i-i-i-pe works.'

Pike had sat bolt upright on Kruud's sofa.

'What fifth pipe!'

She didn't like surprises, especially when they were provided by someone as devious as Sherman H. Kruud. Then she remembered the so-called ventilation pipe in the factory. How could she have been so careless? There was only one thing to do. She would send Polly chasing after Tom. Once she had led her to him, not only would she be able to get rid of the troublesome boy once and for all, she would discover what that fifth pipe was really for.

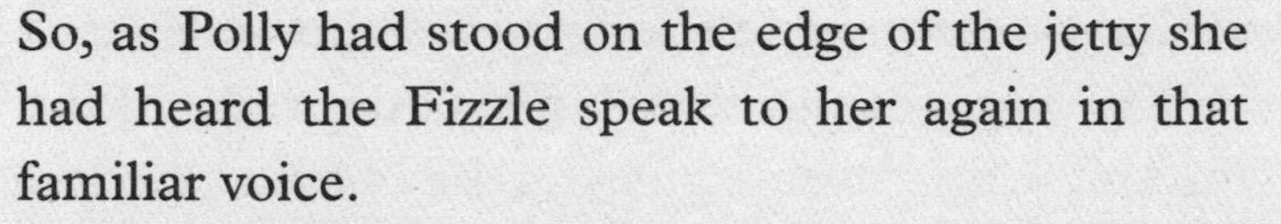

So, as Polly had stood on the edge of the jetty she had heard the Fizzle speak to her again in that familiar voice.

'Follow Tom,' it had commanded. 'Only you can sssstop him from ssssabotaging our plans.'

And she had obeyed instantly. Now Pike was back on her feet. She needed to get back to the factory.

'Driver!' she called out. '*Driver*!'

The butler appeared in the doorway.

'I'm afraid your driver's no longer here, madam,' he explained. 'He's attending to Mr Kruud's other guests.'

'Other guests! What other guests?'

'I'm afraid I couldn't say, madam. They arrived a

few minutes ago aboard Mr Kruud's yacht. They're on their way to the bottling factory.'

'Take me there, now!' Pike demanded.

The butler hesitated.

'I'm afraid I'm about to take Arthur to the mainland for his yearly whisker-trim, madam,' he replied nervously. 'The yacht's waiting for me.'

Immediately Pike's heels clicked over to the doorway. She raised a clawed hand to his face.

'I'm afraid this, I'm afraid that,' she mocked, her blood-red fingernails poised like daggers in front of him. 'These are what you should really be afraid of, you withered old fool.'

The butler's head shrank towards his collar.

'My buggy's just outside,' he quivered. 'Please take it.'

Return of the Frogmen

Unlike the pipe's previous passenger, who had been sucked unwillingly in by his feet, Polly had dived in head first with her Fizzlestick stretched out in front of her. So, when she reached the other end and shot into the Fizzle Filter, she had risen straight and true to the top with barely a kick. She broke the surface with breath to spare, and looked around. The water level had risen so that the roof – or 'lid' as Tom had come to think of it – was within touching distance of her Fizzlestick.

She was about to reach up and give it a tap when she heard voices. She could see that she was alone in the water, yet the voices were loud and clear. She looked up and, gradually, as her eyes became accustomed to the shadow cast by the roof, she began to see figures moving around through its dark mesh surface. Clearly they couldn't see her in the water below, because they were laughing and joking, albeit in languages which Polly couldn't understand. Slowly and quietly she began to swim towards the edge of the tank. When she reached it a few minutes later she hooked the end of her Fizzlestick over the rim. Then she pulled herself up and peered over the side. A hundred feet below, Tom sat dripping and dejected in a pool of Fizzle. Beside him stood a single bamboo-master, making adjustments to a control panel set into the wall. Polly looked for a way down and spotted the top of the metal ladder some distance to her right. She lowered herself back into the water and swam towards it. When she reached it she hooked her Fizzlestick over the rim and prepared to climb over the edge. She reached up and grasped the top of the ladder. Then she stopped. She had felt a small vibration in the metal, just enough to tell her that someone had stepped on to the ladder. Quickly she withdrew her hand and pressed her ear to the inside of the tank. Then she heard it – the slow, rhythmic clunk-clunk-clunk of the person climbing up the other side. And as the sound of the footsteps grew louder, so too did the familiar voice wheezing merrily along to them.

Clunk clunk clunk clunk
'Praise ye mighty dollar'
Clunk
'Praise ye mighty pound'
Clunk
'When I hear them rattle'
Clunk
'I sure do love the sound'
Clunk
'Praise ye mighty dollar'
Clunk
'Praise ye mighty buck'
Clunk
'I've got more than anyone
I can't believe my luck'
Clunk clunk clunk clunk . . .

Eventually the top of Kruud's hat appeared above the rim. Polly shrank quietly back into the water and pressed herself into the side. She closed her eyes, hoping the Fizzle would explain to her what Kruud was up to, to reassure her that this was somehow part of the Fizzle's grand plan. But no such reassurance came, as though the Fizzle itself no longer trusted him. Knowing that even the ripple of a heartbeat could give her away, she took a long, deep breath, filling her lungs as though they were two inflatable lifebelts inside her chest. Then she hung motionless in the dark water as the surface settled, calm and flat, around her. Above her Kruud's face appeared in the gap. He peered over her head towards the centre of the tank.

'Good,' he muttered quietly. 'Even fuller than my piggy bank.' Then he called down to the ground, 'Let's get this show on the road, boy! We got some gas-guzzlin' to do.'

Gas guzzlin'? Suddenly Tom and the others seemed to have a point. Kruud *had* lied to them.

Without warning the roof began to inch downwards towards the rim of the tank. There had been a gap of only about a metre to start with. If Polly was to escape she would have to squeeze through the gap before it closed. But Kruud was still on the ladder, climbing the last few rungs slowly so that as the roof lowered he could step straight on to it. Polly raised herself to peep out. His feet were directly in front of her nose. Come onnnnn . . . If the roof closed with her inside there would be no escape. Then, as he raised one foot to the next rung ready to step on to the roof, Polly decided that she could wait no longer. Lifting herself up as quietly as she could, she leant over the rim of the tank, grabbing the rung directly below Kruud's trailing foot with her right hand and swinging her leg out to catch the ladder further down. Then, as he stepped on to the roof she swung herself fully on to the ladder, pulling her

Fizzlestick clear of the tank just as the roof sealed it shut. But, to her surprise, the roof didn't stop there. It continued on, slowly pushing its way down inside the tank towards the surface of the water, where the process of squeezing the gas upwards into the glass dome would begin. Polly climbed to the top of the ladder and looked across the roof. Kruud was ahead of her, striding confidently towards the dome. If she could follow along behind him, perhaps she could get close enough to see who was inside, or hear what they were saying.

She slipped silently on to the roof and followed him, leaving a watery trail behind her. The dome was brightly lit inside, so it was a while before its occupants saw Kruud approaching. As he stepped inside and closed the door behind him, Polly crouched still and silent, hoping to hear what Kruud was saying. She would have to sneak closer. She edged forward, then crouched down again as Kruud and his guests moved to their seats. Kruud flopped down with his back to her, talking to the two men opposite him. If only she could hear . . . She edged closer still, into the pool of light cast by the dome itself. Then her luck ran out. One of the men looked up and saw her. For a moment he did nothing. Polly realised that he had no idea who she was, or why she was there. She knew also that she was far nearer the door to the dome – and the key which Kruud had left in it – than the ladder. So she stood up straight and waved to the man, striding forward confidently as though she were one of Kruud's most trusted workers delivering a message. By the time Kruud had twisted round and leapt up from his seat, Polly had turned the lock, jumping back as he began pounding on the door with his fists, snarling silent threats and orders through the reinforced soundproof glass. She backed away, then tucked the key into her pocket and ran back to the ladder. She arrived just in time. The lid had continued to push down so that the rim of the tank was now level with her head. Much higher and she wouldn't have been able to climb up. But years spent climbing trees on the Shipley Manor Estate had trained her well, and two seconds later she was over the rim and tapping her way down the ladder on the other side. Tom was alone now. He looked up angrily, then rattled the chain around his wrist just in case Polly hadn't noticed it. She took the gold key from her pocket.

'I locked up Mr Kruud,' she explained, before squatting down to try the key in Tom's padlock.

'Why did you give me away, Polly – what on earth were you thinking?'

But Polly couldn't answer him. One minute she knew for sure that he was a traitor, the next minute

– like now – she knew he wasn't. He was just Tom. And Kruud was clearly up to something. She was scared that she was going mad. Too scared to tell Tom. If only this key fitted . . .

'Mr Kruud boasted to me about what he's doing,' Tom continued. 'He's turned this tank into a giant Fizzle Filter like the one Seymour built for those two slugs. His friends up there are the same people he warned us about, but he's *with* them, Polly, not *against* them. We've fallen right into his trap. They're going to breathe the gas just like we and Hopper did and then join forces to get anything they want. And they *are* going to bottle up some of the Fizzle, but only enough to feed to their business rivals during meetings so that they can read their minds.'

'But why is the Fizzle letting them do all this?' Polly asked him.

'I don't know,' Tom replied, 'but there must be a reason, there must. The Fizzle is good. I know it is.'

'Yes, but I'm not.' Pike stepped into the doorway, her face twitching with rage. 'Very enlightening, ssssweetie, now stop wasting your time with that key and give it to me.'

Polly handed it to her, then returned to Tom's side.

Tom sniffed the air.

'It's you – you're the other Fizzler,' he said.

'You've breathed in the gas too, haven't you?'

'What else did you expect me to do trapped under Shipley Manor for a month?' she hissed back. 'Read a book?'

'And now Hopper doesn't know how to fly any more? That's wicked!'

'Oh shut up, you stupid brat. The old fool wasn't using it lying flat on his back in that nursing home. Now, let me look at this control box . . . Mmmm, very clever.'

She craned her long wrinkled neck towards the top of the Fizzle Filter.

'*We had a deal, Sherman!*' she screamed, loud enough for the puddle around Tom to ripple. She turned back to the box and started to fiddle with a small dial.

'Now let me ssssee. Ah yes. Pressssssure. Ooh look, it's set on "average". But I don't think there's anything average about my disappointment at being double-crossed by that meringue-munching maggot, do you, children?' She turned the dial round another click. '"High"? Mmmm.' She shook her head. 'Far too tame.' Another click. '"Dangerous"? Still not quite . . . volcanic enough.'

There was one setting left: 'explosive'. She nodded approvingly.

'I think that ssssums up my feelings perfectly,' she said through gritted teeth. 'Besides, if

Sssherman wants to be on top of the world with his new friends instead of me, then who am I to stop him?' She yanked the dial round as far as it would go, then calmly removed one of her stiletto shoes. '*And . . . this . . . is . . . just . . . to . . . stop . . . any . . . one . . . think . . . ing . . . they . . . can . . . turn . . it . . . off!*' she screamed, hammering the pointed heel into the dial until nothing remained of it but a dangling spring.

Breathless, she slid her shoe back on and straightened her wig.

'If you can't get rich . . . get even,' she explained, before bending down to Polly. She looked deep into her eyes for a moment then, suddenly, she reached out and grabbed her arms. Drawing her close she pressed her foul-smelling mouth to Polly's ear.

'You remember the voice of the Fizzle, don't you, ssssweetie?' she hissed quietly.

Polly nodded.

'Then come with me.'

She took Polly's hand and led her, unprotesting, towards the door. Tom reached out for his friend, pulling the chain tight against his wrist.

'Polly. Polly! Don't go with her. She's not the Fizzle. She's Venetia Pike. She's hypnotised you, don't you see?'

But Polly couldn't see. The Fizzle had spoken to

her again, filling her head with the barking, clucking, braying sound of certainty that left no room for doubt. She didn't know why the Fizzle wanted her to go with Pike. Only that she had to. She turned back to Tom, smiling.

'It's what the Fizzle wants,' she explained.

The corridor outside stretched full circle around the chamber. Pike led Polly through the door and turned left, just in time to pass a dozen bamboo-masters on their way to investigate the Captain's breakout. They didn't have far to go. The Captain, Slugbucket and Maggie had already followed the pipe to the upper level and were running along the corridor towards them.

'Polly!' the Captain called, but Pike was already pulling her away towards the exit behind the wall of bamboo-masters that now blocked the Captain's path. The Captain stopped and looked for a way round them. There was none. Worse still, a dozen frogmen had appeared behind them, blocking their escape. The Captain and Slugbucket turned themselves back to back either side of Maggie, bracing themselves for a fight from whichever direction it came. The Captain's hand went to the hilt of his sword, ready to draw it out to defend his shipmates. But neither the bamboo-masters nor the frogmen were deterred. They continued to advance slowly from both sides.

'Let's be 'avin' yer, then,' growled Slugbucket, rolling up his sleeves.

The frogmen were the first to grant him his wish. They ran forward. But instead of attacking them, as he and his shipmates had expected, they split into two groups and passed either side of them. Then, equally mysteriously, the frogmen regrouped to form a protective barrier between them and Kruud's bamboo-masters. And just in time. Under orders to capture the Shipley Manor crew the bamboo-masters suddenly charged forward, intent on reaching them. The frogmen took the brunt of the blow, bravely blocking their path to the Captain and his shipmates as though their lives depended on it. But one bamboo-master, faster and stronger than the rest, broke through the tangled scrum of bodies and raced towards Maggie. Before she could reach her, one of Slugbucket's great arms knocked the girl sideways. He lifted Moolah off her feet and pinned her against the wall.

'Don't you dare lift a finger 'gainst Maggie,' he said.

Moolah shook her head.

'I want to help you.'

Maggie stepped up to her.

'Where are the children?' she demanded.

'I can take you to them,' Moolah replied.

Slugbucket snorted.

'I've drunk the special water,' she continued. 'Mr Kruud told me to throw the bottle away but I drank some. Please, I want to help.'

Slugbucket glanced at the Captain, then lowered her to the ground.

'This way, quickly,' she said.

By now the fight had moved back towards the chamber. As they approached the entrance Moolah pushed a surprised-looking Luka out of the way and ushered them inside.

'Tom!'

Moolah ran over to Tom and unlocked him.

'The Fizzle's going to explode,' he told them. 'We have to get all the children off the island.'

The Captain held up his hand.

'What children, Tom?'

So Tom explained as fast as he could – about Kruud and his accomplices trapped on top of the Fizzle Filter, about how Pike had sabotaged the controls and about the army of child slaves curled up in their oil drums outside, unaware of the danger they were in. As his words tumbled out the Captain's jaw dropped further and further towards his boots. How in the name of Neptune had he managed to steer his crew to such a place? And why had the Fizzle encouraged him? He looked up at the tank, shaking his head. From now on the Fizzle could do what it liked. He was the Captain of Shipley Manor, not the Fizzle, and the safety of its crew was his responsibility, and his alone. What a nautical numbskull he'd been. He turned to Moolah.

'How do we get out of here?'

'There's a door on the other side of the tank,' she replied, pulling Tom to his feet. 'Follow me.'

She led them around the outside of the huge Fizzle Filter and through an exit into the corridor on the other side. Facing them, a pair of double doors led on to the mountainside. They stepped through just as the sun was rising, row by row turning the oil barrels at the bottom of the track bright orange. Speeding past them towards the runway were Pike and, motionless beside her in the golf buggy, Polly.

'This way,' said Moolah. Instead of running down the winding track, she leaped off the edge and began sliding down the mountain on her backside. The Captain and the others followed, but by the time they reached the bottom Pike had already smashed through the gates and driven through, leaving them flapping wide open. Moolah, suddenly alarmed, accelerated towards them like a greyhound let out of its trap, dragging her cane along the oil drums as she ran, and barking the familiar early morning wake-up call: 'Up up up up up up up . . .'

She reached the gates in time, slamming them shut just as two alligators prepared to amble through in search of breakfast. Behind her, a thousand sleepy heads rose obediently out of their slumbers and appeared over the tops of the drums. The Captain and the others caught up a few seconds later.

'Let me through the gates,' the Captain demanded. 'I'll take my chances.'

Moolah barred his way.

'You won't make it on foot. You'll need this.' She nodded behind him. The Captain turned to see Pepe and Paco approaching in a golf buggy. When they reached him the two boys jumped out, leaving the engine humming. The Captain looked around at the sea of bemused young faces staring at them. Then he looked up at the side of the volcano.

'Slugbucket, if the Fizzle does explode, rocks are going to fall like hailstones all over the island. I want you and our friends here to evacuate the children. As far as I can see,' he said, scanning the alligator-infested swampland in front of him, 'Shipley Manor is the only way to get them off the island. Get the children on board as fast as you can, then sail the house to a safe distance. Smash through that damn security grille if you have to.'

Then the Captain and Maggie climbed into the buggy, with Tom in the back, and Moolah opened the gates to let them pass through.

They sped along the runway in pursuit of Pike. The alligators, familiar with the to-ings and fro-ings of the buggies, didn't disturb them, and they reached the gates at the opposite end. These opened and closed automatically as they passed through. As they approached Kruud's villa Tom saw Polly disappear through a side arch on to the terrace beyond. He leaped out of the buggy and chased after her, but as he arrived on the terrace he froze in his tracks. To his left, near the house, stood the pilot he had first seen on his train journey down to the docks many weeks before. Without the hat and goggles, which had been removed, Tom understood finally why the pilot had seemed so familiar to him. It was Hopper. Or rather someone who looked like Hopper but with a mass of the familiar red curls cascading down to her shoulders. Scarlett, Hopper's great-granddaughter. It had to be. She too was frozen where she stood, her eyes fixed not on Pike, who stood smiling menacingly in the middle of the terrace, but beyond her to the low wall on the edge of the cliff. There, standing on top of it with nothing but a thousand feet of sheer cliff face between her and the rocks below, was

Polly. The Captain and Maggie skidded to a halt alongside Tom.

Pike raised her hand.

'Don't come any closer,' she warned them. 'I was just explaining to your friend here . . .' She nodded towards Scarlett. '. . . that Polly and I have a sssspecial understanding. Sssstep a little closer to the edge, would you, Polly, just to sssshow the Captain and your mother what I mean?'

Polly shuffled forward so that her toes were poking out over the precipice. Maggie clamped her hand over her mouth to stop herself from screaming.

'Tom knows what I can do, don't you?'

Tom nodded. The Captain looked at him, puzzled.

'We have to do as she says,' Tom told him. 'She can make Polly do whatever she wants. That's why she's been behaving so strangely since we left Portsmouth.'

The Captain looked ready to explode.

'If anything happens to Polly, I'll . . .'

'You'll do what, you barnacled buffoon – sing a sea shanty? Polly won't jump unless anything happens to me or I tell her to. Isn't that right, Polly?'

Polly nodded.

'And you *will* tell me if anyone comes near you,

won't you?'

She nodded again.

'Good, then I think I'll help myself to Sherman's rather sssplendid jet – a little compenssssation for all my hard work. Let's face it,' she added, taking the gold key from her pocket and hurling it over the cliff edge, 'no one can ssssave him now, so he won't be needing it any more.'

Pike strode past them towards Kruud's plane, pausing only to kick a bucket of stinking fish guts into the middle of his crystal-blue swimming pool. Then, a minute later, the automatic gates closed behind her and she was on her way. As the plane cleared the runway and set out over the ocean, the first small rupture in the side of the Fizzle Filter sent a jet of water smashing through the side of the volcano, hurling a huge chunk of jagged rock high into the air. It headed straight for Polly but dropped short, landing like a meteorite on the empty jetty below, catapulting a forest of broken, splintered wood halfway up the cliff face. Maggie stepped towards Polly, but Tom pulled her back. Polly turned to her.

'I'll jump, if the Fizzle tells me to,' she reminded her, quite matter-of-factly. Then she turned back and continued to gaze blankly into space.

Suddenly, the Fizzle punched another hole in the tank, firing a second unstoppable jet of water through the chamber wall and sending more debris hurtling into the air. This time a small, whistling fragment landed just a few metres away from Polly, breaking off a section of the terrace wall. Polly watched unconcerned as it tumbled towards the water below. Again Maggie stepped forward, only for Tom and the Captain to grab her.

'I'm the only one who can save Polly,' Tom said, 'but you have to promise not to go near her.'

The Captain and Maggie exchanged glances. The Captain nodded. Tom sat down against the wall, closed his eyes and began counting backwards. He imagined himself as the kite, flying over the rooftops. Only this time he headed out past Hopper's windsock, flying over houses he'd never seen before. He was looking for something special – a house that reminded him of Pike. Perhaps it would be built with pink bricks and have a white-blonde thatched roof to match her wig. Or maybe it teetered on top of stilts as she did on her high-heeled stiletto shoes. But instead he found himself flying over rows of ordinary terraced houses each of which looked identical. Perhaps his plan wouldn't work. Perhaps Pike's mind lay in the opposite direction, or had already passed beneath him unnoticed. Then a clue reached his nostrils – that same familiar smell of rotting fish that seemed to follow Pike wherever she went. He concentrated on the smell, following the scent like a bloodhound. Eventually it led him to a plain front door, in the centre of which was a letterbox. He bent down to peer through it and immediately the smell invaded his nostrils. This was the place all right. He had found the way into Pike's mind. He pushed the door and it opened with a faint hiss. At his feet just inside the entrance lay a doormat, beyond which a thick cream-coloured carpet led to a door at the end of the hallway. So far everything about it seemed, well, normal. Tom looked down at the doormat. 'Welcome' it said, just like his doormat at home.

So, just like at home, he stepped on to it to wipe his feet.

Hot and Cold

He couldn't remember falling through the trapdoor. All Tom knew was that the moment he stepped on to the doormat it had vanished from underneath him and that now he was somewhere else. Somewhere cold and damp and, worst of all, completely dark. He stretched his arms out in front of him and edged forward. A few paces ahead a bluish glow appeared in the middle of the thick, curling fog which Tom could now see lay all around him. He felt a sudden surge of confidence as he realised that the fog was making his skin tingle. That meant only one thing. Fizzle. It was there, wrapped around him like a misty blanket, and it was trying to show him a way through the darkness.

He edged towards the light. It led him to the foot of a high wall whose smooth black surface curved away into the darkness either side of him. The fog continued to glow, licking the wall's surface to reveal thousands of dark, interlocking panels which covered it like the scales of an enormous fish. Tom touched one of them nervously with his fingertips. Instantly it came to life like a television screen, revealing the image of a young Venetia Pike dropping a worm into the lunchbox of a small, unsuspecting schoolboy sitting next to her in the playground. Tom recognised her victim straightaway – it was Barclay Grub, his father's crooked ex-boss at Shipley Bank. He pressed another panel to find Pike stealing sweets out of Grub's blazer pocket. On to the next and there she was again, sprinkling drawing pins on to her teacher's chair. Tom had found his way into Pike's memory, where every moment of her wicked and dishonest life was stored. Unfortunately, it wasn't the part of her mind he was looking for.

He pressed two panels simultaneously. Using the extra light cast by their flickering screens he began to make out another wall behind him, which meant that he was standing inside a long, curving corridor. With no doors visible in either wall, it occurred to him that, given Pike's devious, twisted mind, he might be standing inside an enormous maze. Either way, although his plan was simple, carrying it out clearly wouldn't be. His idea was to find the flying skill which Pike had so cruelly stolen from Hopper, and threaten to steal it back from her. He would point out that, as she was currently at the controls of Kruud's plane high above the ocean, suddenly losing the ability to fly would almost certainly result in her death. Pike would know he was right, and the fear of plummeting thousands of feet to a watery grave would, Tom hoped, force her to release Polly from her hypnotic grip. But he would have to find the skill first. Where would she keep something so precious, where no one else would be able to find it? If her mind was indeed a maze, then there was only one place. The centre. Tom's heart sank. He'd never been any good at finding his way through mazes, let alone in semi-darkness. Still, he had to try. He waited for a moment, hoping the Fizzle would show him which way to go, but it didn't. Instead, as Tom set off briskly along the wall with no idea where he was heading, the glow seemed content to travel with him, lighting rather than guiding his way.

But after a while he noticed that the light had changed colour. The difference was very slight, but he was sure that the glow, even though it was still blue, had become paler, more . . . icy. Then he remembered the hide-and-seek game Polly liked to play with him. She would hide an object, usually something really annoying like one of his shoes, and demand that he search for it.

'Warm,' she would declare, fanning her face, if he was heading in the right direction.

'C-c-c-cold,' she would warn him, shivering, if he went the wrong way.

And what did he do whenever she said that? He looked in the opposite direction of course. Tom turned around and began to run as fast as he could the other way. The foggy glow kept pace with him as he hurtled along the twisting, turning corridor. Watching it from the corner of his eye he noticed the light begin, slowly but unmistakably, to change colour from blue to purple. When it turns red, he thought, I'll know I'm nearly there. Suddenly the walls either side of him separated left and right. Another lay directly in front of him to create a T-junction. He stopped briefly to catch his breath, then turned left and ran down another dark, winding corridor, carefully watching the colour speeding through the fog at his side. He had chosen well. The fog continued to glow purple and was even now, he thought, becoming tinged with red at the edges. At the next junction he turned right, running along for several seconds before realising his mistake and heading back the way he had come. Then left, then right again, and along at full sprint until the patch of fog beside him was glowing like a red-hot poker. Then, suddenly, the wall ended.

Ahead of him, rising like a shadow out of the misty darkness in the centre of the maze, stood a perfect replica of the bandstand in Shipley town square. As he stepped towards it, something on the wall beside him caught his eye. He turned, almost jumping out of his skin as he found himself staring at his own reflection. At first he thought he must be staring into a circular mirror. He moved to the left, expecting his reflection to disappear. Instead, it followed him. So he moved to the right. The same thing happened. Instantly his legs turned to jelly as he realised that he wasn't staring into a mirror at all. He was staring into an eye the size of a dustbin lid. Worse still, the eye was staring back at him. Suddenly he knew why the walls of the maze had curved so smoothly, why they were covered in millions of scales and why, when he had touched them, they had felt alive under his hand. The walls weren't walls at all. They were the sides of giant snakes, whose bodies formed the twists and turns of the maze and whose ghostly, red-tinged heads he could just make out through the fog, forming a protective circle around the bandstand. Slowly he backed away from the eye towards the centre of the maze, watching his reflection follow him. Then, as the snake's mouth hissed open to reveal a pair of fangs hanging down like huge dripping stalactites, he turned and ran. Alerted to his presence, the other snakes writhed into life and converged on the bandstand, just as Tom hurled himself up the steps. At the top the snake nearest him lashed out with its tongue, catching Tom's ankle and tripping him over. Tom tumbled to the floor but managed to keep rolling until he reached the centre. Then he leaped up into a crouching position, turning slowly, wondering which snake would attack him first.

But the snakes didn't follow him inside. Instead, they stared at him, hissing angrily, their eyes flaring like spotlights, flooding the bandstand with light and blinding Tom to everything outside. Tom shielded his eyes and looked around him. At once he understood why the snakes hadn't forced their way into the bandstand. Its contents were too precious to risk disturbing. Around its perimeter, leaving only the narrow gap through which Tom had scrambled, hundreds of display stands were arranged three deep – the tallest at the back, the shortest at the front – so that the glass specimen jars perched on top of each one could clearly be seen. Each jar contained one of Pike's skills. But unlike Hopper she hadn't stored them as sweets. Instead, Pike's dastardly abilities were stored in the form of grotesque, distorted creatures that no one would ever want to hold, let alone eat. Tom looked in horror at the warped collection of venomous spiders, poisonous snakes and deadly scorpions that wriggled and writhed inside the glass jars. He forced himself up close to read the label on the outside of a jar containing a double-headed snake. '*Serpens duplicitus*: two-faced double dealing,' it read. She's an expert at that all right, he thought. The specimen next to it was even more disgusting. Although it looked like a spider, its legs were – Tom looked closer before recoiling in disgust – fingers. '*Digitus strangulo*,' said the label. 'Finger-fighting'. Quickly he moved to the next jar, whose occupant – a fluffy pink rabbit with floppy, folded-down ears – looked far more cuddly. It cocked its head cutely to one side and blinked at Tom with its huge saucer-like eyes. Tom leaned forward to read the label – '*Innocens deceptius*: ambushing' – but before he had time to move away a huge mouthful of razor-sharp teeth lunged for his face. As they crashed against the glass Tom stumbled back, almost knocking over the jar next to him. He managed to catch it mid-wobble, then steadied it back on its stand before bending down to read the label: '*Escorpio verticus*: flying.' He'd found it! But his joy was short-lived. When he looked through the glass he discovered that Hopper's flying skill was now stored inside something that was not only too revolting to eat, but far too big – a huge, winged scorpion. Twice the size of a rat and ten times as fearsome, its glistening black pincers snapped together like garden shears whilst, above its body, the venom-filled sting on the end of its tail hovered like a pin-sharp knitting needle, ready to spear its next victim. Tom swallowed hard. Clearly, eating it was out of the question, so how could he persuade Pike that he was in a position to steal the skill contained within it? Then the answer came to him, even though the thought of it terrified him. He lifted the lid and, suddenly, the hissing outside stopped. From the gullet of one of the snakes a stick-like figure emerged to stand in its open mouth. Although the figure was invisible to Tom behind the curtain of white light surrounding the bandstand, its voice was unmistakable – Pike.

'If you hadn't already noticcccced, I'm busy flying a plane,' she said.

'Let Polly go,' Tom demanded, blinking into the light, 'or you won't be flying it for much longer.'

'Really, and how do you intend sssstopping me, sssweetie – are you going to sssswallow that sssscorpion whole or spend the next ssssix months chewing it to death? I know,' she added, mockingly, 'maybe you can pull its ssssting out and use it as a toothpick.'

'I'll let it sting me,' Tom replied, placing a trembling hand over the jar. 'Its venom will pass into me along with your ability to fly. And then you'll crash.'

Pike hesitated.

'You wouldn't dare,' she snarled.

'Yes, I would,' Tom replied, lowering his hand closer. 'Polly can't stay on the wall any longer – she'll be killed if I don't.'

'Get out now,' Pike barked, her voice appearing to get closer, 'and I may sssspare her. Otherwise I'll make her jump.'

'No,' said Tom firmly, his hand now almost touching the rim of the jar. 'Let her go now or I'll let it sting me. You'll crash before you can do anything about it.'

Pike seemed to hesitate. So, shaking with fear, Tom lowered his hand even closer to the scorpion.

Suddenly, a dark shape pierced the wall of light in front of him and Pike, her arms outstretched, hurled herself at him like a spear, pushing him away from the jar. As he fell backwards a sharp, white-hot pain punctured the palm of his hand. He landed heavily on his back, closing his eyes as the back of his head hit the floorboards a split second later. Then, before he could recover a hard slap cracked across the side of his face.

'Tom, wake up. You've done it. I'm safe.'

He opened his eyes to find himself back on Kruud's terrace. Polly was bent over him, her arm raised ready to slap him again.

'Ouch!' he said, rubbing his cheek. 'Whose side are you on?'

'Yours, of course, silly.'

'Well, it's about time,' replied Tom, grinning. 'At least you won't have to wear pink any more.'

He sat up and inspected his hand. There was no puncture wound in it but it was throbbing painfully as it pumped a cold, prickly feeling around his body. Tom looked across at Scarlett's plane parked at the end of the runway. She was already running towards the cockpit, beckoning for them to follow, but as the prickle finally reached his toes Tom knew, beyond any doubt, that he could fly the plane too. Clearly Hopper's flying skills had passed to him and, judging by the suddenness of Polly's release, Pike hadn't survived long without them.

The Captain pulled Tom to his feet just as a large chunk of rock landed against the balcony wall, demolishing the section where Polly had been standing only moments before.

'We have to go,' he said. 'Fizzle's bursting out all over the place. I only hope Slugbucket's managed to get those children to safety.'

Scarlett was already revving the seaplane's engine as the Captain clambered into the seat beside her, and Polly, Tom and Maggie jumped into the back. Moments later they were airborne, skimming over the gates at the other end of the runway before circling high above the cave. As Fizzle continued to puncture the side of the volcano, hurling rocks and debris into the air, it was clear that Shipley Manor was still trapped inside, behind the security grille. Worse still, large rocks had fallen into the sea around the cave mouth, so that even if Shipley Manor were able to break out it would be trapped at the base of the volcano, unable to escape the avalanche of rocks that almost certainly would sink it.

'Calypso!' cried Polly, looking down through tear-streaked eyes as another rock fell to block her baby sister's route to safety. 'Slugbucket! Seymour!' She fell sobbing into her mother's arms. All along it was she who had been tricked, not Tom. Everything was her fault.

'Drop me off as near to the cave mouth as you can, Scarlett,' bellowed the Captain above the roar of the engine. 'Then take the others to a safe distance and wait for me there. And no, Tom,' he said, leaning over his shoulder, 'you're not coming too. If I lose you a second time I'll never be able to look your father in the face again.'

Scarlett circled one more time, then landed her plane a hundred metres from the semicircle of rocks that lay around the cave mouth. Evidently Fizzle was still being sucked into the cave, because the moment the plane touched the surface the current started to pull it towards the rocks. Scarlett revved the engine to hold it steady whilst the Captain stepped out on to the float. Then with a brief backward glance to the others, he jumped into the water.

For a moment Tom remained in his seat. Exhausted and wet, he wanted nothing more than to obey the Captain's order. Polly was safe beside him now and he knew that no one was better able to sail Shipley Manor to safety than the Captain himself. Neither had he ever felt more at home. Every sound, and smell, and vibration inside the plane was familiar, every gauge and dial a trusted friend. And yet, as the plane slowly gathered pace to return to the air, he knew he couldn't stay. If the Captain couldn't find a way to sail Shipley Manor through those rocks, then what would he do? He would need help.

So, as droplets of water began to streak towards the edges of the windscreen Tom quietly slipped out of the door and jumped after him. Polly screamed and instinctively tried to follow. But this time Maggie was too quick for her, tightening her grip around her howling daughter until the plane was airborne.

The Fizzle's Great Escape

The last of the Fizzle was flowing towards the cave. Despite being a weak swimmer, Tom knew that he merely had to stay afloat and let the current do the rest. Sure enough it carried him along, picking up speed as it was funnelled through narrow gaps in the rocks, before slamming Tom into the security grille just a few seconds after the Captain. Several Fizzlefish were there too, pinned flat against the crisscrossed metal by the force of water passing through it. Further down, others, having succumbed finally to the current, were streaking under the grille like dashes of watery paint, just a vertical pipe ride away from their new home inside Kruud's giant Fizzle Filter.

The Captain looked at Tom sternly.

'Disobeying orders, shipmate,' he observed, plucking a strand of seaweed from his beard, 'but as you're here I think we'd better get on with it, don't you?'

Tom nodded.

'On the count of three, then – one, two, three.'

They each took a deep breath and ducked below the surface, pushing themselves down until the current swept them under the grille. As they surfaced on the other side Tom could see that Seymour had raised the drawbridge and turned Shipley Manor to face the ocean. But despite the froth being churned up by the paddle-wheels, the house was stationary, balanced perfectly against the current. Having been in the water before Tom could tell that the flow was weakening. Perhaps they had a chance. He and the Captain let the Fizzle carry them safely past the spinning paddle-wheels before swimming across to the jetty. Then they climbed up and ran back towards the house, which stood just a few feet away from the side.

Suddenly the ends of two thick ropes thumped on to the jetty beside them. Tom looked up to discover that they'd been thrown down by two frogmen. Then Slugbucket's face appeared between them.

'It's all roight, Cap'n,' he called down, 'they're friends o' someone called Scarlett. Reckon they've been tryin' to warn us 'bout Kruud all along. Jus' hang on tight.'

Tom and the Captain grabbed the ropes and swung out to the house. Then two lines of frogmen began hauling them up the side of the building. As they rose past each floor, children crowded round the portholes, pressing their faces up against the glass to peer out at them. Clearly, Shipley Manor had a full cargo. At the top Slugbucket reached out and pulled them on to the roof, before slapping the two nearest frogmen on the back.

'Noice work, lads. Now, if I were you I'd check those kids are settled down tight – I reckons we're in fer a bumpy ride . . .' As they turned to leave he pulled Nautipus out of his jacket. 'Oh, an' take ol' cowardy custard 'ere with you – he'll be safer down there too.'

Then he, Tom and the Captain quickly made their way to the conservatory. Seymour was sitting in front of the ship's wheel with Calypso still perched on his knees. She turned and saw the Captain first.

'Ooooh,' she said, clapping her hands.

Seymour, his brow beaded with sweat, was even more pleased to see him.

'The current's too strong,' he reported, moving aside immediately. 'Even on full power we couldn't get out, so I've just been keeping the house steady waiting for it to weaken.'

'Thank you, shipmate,' the Captain said, taking the wheel just as a rock the size of an armchair crashed into the water in front of them.

'It's weakening all right, but so is the roof by the look of it. I don't think we can afford to wait any longer.'

'But how are we going to get past the rocks outside?' Tom asked him. 'I couldn't see a gap wide enough.'

'We'll just have to smash our way through them, Tom. Like an icebreaker. These walls are made of solid stone, don't forget. Besides, what other choice do we have?'

Suddenly Calypso made a grab for the bottle sticking out of Tom's back pocket. Of course! He'd forgotten all about it. He snapped round to Seymour.

'You remember your idea of using Fizzle bubbles to fly around the world?'

Seymour nodded.

'How much concentrated Flying Formula did you make?'

Seymour's face flushed red.

'Well, probably more than I needed,' he admitted. 'I thought Edna might like to come along, and then there's my mother, and I know my brother and his two daughters would jump at the chance . . .'

'Yes, but how *much*?' Tom repeated.

'About a dozen barrels of it,' Seymour told him. 'They're outside, by Slugbucket's caravan. Why?'

But Tom was no longer there. He had already grabbed Slugbucket and was leading him as fast as he could across the roof, ducking nervously each time a rumble threatened to send rocks falling around their heads. They found Seymour's barrels lined up against the wall.

'We need to empty them over the side,' said Tom. He looked back to see that Seymour had followed them. 'All except one,' he added.

'No!' said Seymour. 'I know what you're doing, Tom. You have to empty it *all* in – every drop.'

'But what about your plan to . . .?'

'Every last drop,' Seymour insisted. 'Now!'

'Roight y'are, Seymour,' Slugbucket said, bending down with Tom to grab the first barrel. But it was as thick as a tree trunk and twice as heavy.

'I'm gettin' on a bit, ya know,' he grunted, as the barrel failed to budge. 'We're goin' to need 'elp.'

As he spoke a dozen frogmen appeared back on the roof.

'Bloimey, that was quick. Roight then, lads, we need to empty this lot into the water pronto.'

Without a word the frogmen rushed over and set

about the task, three to a barrel, lifting and tipping their contents over the side of the building in long, splashy waterfalls. Tom looked over the edge. The pumps had stopped and along with it the current. As ordinary seawater settled back into the cave, the paddle-wheels started to bite, mixing the formula in with it but, at the same time, inching Shipley Manor towards the entrance. And still Tom had no idea how he was going to raise the security grille. He needed more time.

He left the others to finish emptying the barrels and raced back to the conservatory.

'Captain, you have to wait for us to open the security grille.'

'There isn't time, Tom,' he replied, as another overhead explosion rocked the house from side to side. 'The roof might collapse any moment. We'll just have to break it down.' He increased the power.

'But I have an idea,' Tom protested. 'The Fizzle can . . .'

But the Captain shook his head firmly.

'We've trusted the Fizzle all along, Tom, and just look where it's led us. I'm sorry, shipmate. We're leaving.'

As the paddle-wheels began to bite deeper into the water Tom looked ahead in dismay as the security grille loomed closer and closer to them.

Even if he had the key there was no time for him to open it now. There was nothing he could do.

Suddenly another piece of the cave roof crashed down, landing beside the door leading on to the jetty. Tom rushed outside to see Moolah standing in the doorway, a small boy clinging, barefoot and terrified, to her back. The impact had left a gaping hole in front of the bamboo-master but she jumped it with ease and sprinted along the jetty towards the house, pursued by a chain of smaller rocks which ripped up the planks behind her, filling the air with noise and flying splinters. Slugbucket had spotted her too and thrown down a rope. Moolah grabbed it, then looked up to see Tom at Slugbucket's side, frantically waving to her and stabbing his finger towards the security grille. Moolah understood straightaway, and with the tiny child still stuck like a limpet to her back she dropped the rope and ran to the metal steps at the side of the cave mouth. Leaping up two at a time, she quickly reached the walkway at the top and ran to the control panel in the centre. She pulled the key chain from her belt and began passing the keys through her fingers. She glanced quickly over her shoulder. Shipley Manor was just metres away from the grille now, edging slowly but surely towards it. Then she found the right one. In a flash she thrust it into the lock and turned it, before slamming her hand against the control button.

Slowly, the enormous security grille began to rise. Then, as its base lifted clear of the water Tom saw exactly what he had hoped to see – a thin film of quivering Fizzle Flying Formula being drawn up behind it like a vast liquid window pane. As he and Slugbucket raced up to the Crow's Nest more rocks fell, demolishing what was left of the jetty and shattering the solar panels on the conservatory roof. Shards of red glass fell on to the Captain's shoulders. But he stood firm at the wheel, setting both paddle-wheels to full power and steering straight ahead. Then, even before the security grille reached the top of the cave mouth, Shipley Manor began to push through it into the early morning sunlight. Tom and Slugbucket watched from the Crow's Nest walkway as, below them, the Fizzle skin stretched itself over Shipley Manor's bow. Tom crossed his fingers.

'Please don't break, *please* don't break.'

The bottom edge of the security grille was level with Tom's nose now, but the top of the Crow's Nest was several feet above him. If it hit the grille the giant hoop that he'd created would be broken and his plan would fail. The grille just needed to rise a few more feet, but it seemed to be lifting so slowly. Come on, come onnnn . . .

And then it was up, just as the Crow's Nest

began to pass underneath it. But Tom's relief was short-lived, as he and Slugbucket turned their attention to Moolah and the small boy stranded above the cave mouth. With the jetty destroyed they all knew what had to be done. Moolah took her lucky golf ball out of her pocket and pressed it into the child's hand. Then she leaned over the railings and dangled him as far as she could over the edge. The boy looked down, his eyes and mouth wide open in terror as, several metres below on the Crow's Nest walkway, Slugbucket prepared to catch him. Finally, with a nod to Slugbucket, Moolah let the boy drop and he fell, screaming, into Slugbucket's outstretched arms. Then it was the bamboo-master's turn. She swung herself out over the edge, ready to jump. It was a long way down, with nothing but the narrow Crow's Nest walkway to aim for. And it was moving, slowly disappearing through the cave mouth like a sun setting beneath the horizon.

'Come on! You have to jump now,' Tom shouted to her.

But Moolah was simply picking her moment. When it arrived she let go, landing as lightly as a cat on the Crow's Nest walkway.

As she stood up, the pressure in the Fizzle Filter two levels above had again reached breaking point. The Fizzle searched for a new way of escape. This time, with the pump halted, the weakest place to release its pent-up energy was not through another hole in the tank. It was back down the pipe. And that's where it went, expanding constantly as it hurtled downwards, before being fired out of the bottom with the force of a missile. As it hit the cave floor the impact opened up a thin crack in the seabed, through which the Fizzle continued boring down hundreds of feet. There it collided with one of the vast interconnecting Fizzle reservoirs that Hopper's research had predicted. But far from diffusing its enormous power, this served only to increase it, as the pressure grew, expanding from one reservoir to another, forcing one bubble into two, two into four, four into sixteen until, within a few seconds, the Fizzle underground had expanded so much that it needed to find a way back to the surface. And the nearest place was Kruud's cave. As Shipley Manor's stern began to pass through the cave mouth the seabed behind it ruptured, pushing up a wave which rolled under the house and lifted it out of the cave. As it emerged the Fizzle skin closed behind it, encasing Shipley Manor in a huge bubble which rose like a majestic silver moon and floated over the rocks that had been blocking their way.

But its flight was a short one. As Shipley Manor passed over into clear water, a fragment of flying debris landed on the roof, bursting the bubble on its way and sending the house crashing down into the ocean. As it landed the water parted around it, pushed outwards like the edges of a bomb crater, before rolling back in again, rising up the walls and threatening to engulf them. But the buoyancy foam that filled the cellar did its job. As Tom and the others held tight the house pushed itself back to the surface. There it settled, surrounded, as Tom observed sadly, by nothing but an ocean of flat, ordinary seawater. But whilst the Fizzle may have finished with them, the Captain could see that it hadn't finished with Dollar Island. So, as rocks and debris continued to fall, the Captain set a speedy course towards Scarlett's plane waiting half a mile away. From there, reunited at last, the crew of Shipley Manor and their new shipmates gathered on the roof to watch in silence as Kruud's bottling plant, and with it Polly and Tom's hopes of completing their mission, came to an abrupt end. In its underground reservoir deep beneath Kruud's cave the ever-expanding Fizzle had, finally, reached the point of no return. As the air around Dollar Island tremored, and the alligators sought sanctuary in the bottom of their swamps, the Fizzle ripped the floor of Kruud's cave wide open and launched itself upwards, bursting straight through into the bottling factory before punching a hole into the Fizzle Filter on the floor above. When the two immense forces collided the Fizzle exploded through the top of the mountain and continued to surge hundreds of feet into the air, like an endless column of froth escaping from a champagne bottle. But, as a shoal of newly liberated Fizzlefish began spiralling back into the sea around them, neither Polly nor Tom felt like celebrating. Hopper's lifelong dream – that the whole world should 'Get the Fizzle' – was over. Or so they thought.

Thousands of miles away on the Shipley Manor estate, Tom's father stepped out of the log cabin into the late afternoon sunlight. The six cabins on the estate had survived the deluge that transported the main house down to the sea and, in Tom's absence, Roger had volunteered to keep them clean once a week after work, until the Captain returned and could decide what to do with them. The Fizzle and the house were gone now, leaving nothing behind them but a deep, dry hole like a moon crater, from which Roger could hear a faint hissing noise. He peered into the bottom and saw that a thin crack had appeared. No sooner had he stepped into the crater to investigate, than the ground began to move under his feet. Quickly he scrambled back out and, as the hiss became a whistle, and the whistle became a roar, he watched as the ground split open and Fizzle burst out of its deep underground reservoir and exploded into the sky. The single jet continued to rise a thousand feet into the air, carried onwards and upwards by the immense force of water pressing up behind it. There it began to disperse, forming a thin, flat cloud which spread itself across the sky like an ever-expanding silver blanket. The supply of Fizzle seemed endless, and as the jet continued to press into its centre so the silvery cloud grew, stretching in every direction as far as Roger could see, and beyond.

The Fizzle was coming out of its slumber. As it expanded under Kruud's volcano, only a fraction of it could find its escape there. The rest hurtled from reservoir to reservoir, spreading the chain reaction underground until there was nowhere else for it to go, except up. As the Fizzle sought out every extinct volcano, fault line and blowhole from which to make its escape so, worldwide, a thousand jets of sparkling water erupted into the sky, before spreading out wide and flat to meet their neighbours. Within a couple of hours the clouds had merged, so that the earth was shrouded in a single, seamless coating of silvery Fizzle. Then, as the midday sun shone down over Dollar Island, the eruptions ceased, and another chain reaction began. As the sunlight hit the Fizzle cloud, so each droplet captured it and spread it to the next, which spread it to the next until, on the other side of the world, the sky lit up and, as night turned suddenly to day, billions of people awoke from their beds to an early dawn.

Around the world, people stepped out from their homes and factories, their offices and their shops. Guns fell silent on the battlefield and squabbling neighbours looked up from their garden fences, as the world craned its neck to gaze goggle-eyed at the silver screen that had appeared above them. From his bed in Room 5 of the Skyview Nursing Home in America, Harry 'Hopper' Hawkins – awake but unable to open his eyes or move – sensed the hubbub. As his visitors left his bedside to join the doctors and nurses staring up at the sky outside, he spoke to Tom from behind his weary eyelids.

'Tell me what's happening, Tom. Is it the Fizzle?'

So, surrounded by his shipmates on top of the Crow's Nest, Tom described to Hopper the events as they unfolded on the silver screen above them.

First there was a flash as, for an instant, the Fizzle turned white. Then, just as suddenly, the cloud turned itself black and plunged the earth into darkness. Birds stopped whistling, and an eerie silence chilled the air. Then a lone speck of light appeared above their heads, hurtling through the darkness towards them. As it grew so Tom began to recognise it. The earth. A perfect mirror image. Closer still and suddenly its great continents filled the sky, before being pushed aside by the blue of the Caribbean Ocean, into which, in turn, another lone speck appeared, this time growing almost instantly into the shape of Dollar Island, and beside it hurtling down on them, Shipley Manor itself, and the Crow's Nest, and then . . .

Tom ducked. They all ducked. But there was no collision. The sky was just a moving picture, after all. And it had paused. He looked up and, like every other person on the earth who gazed up into a mirror image of their own face, he gazed up into his, as though *he* were the centre of the universe. Then, slowly, the image started moving closer again, until one of his eyes filled the sky, its black centre bearing down on him like the entrance to a tunnel, connecting one place to another. Then in a blink he was through it and, suddenly, the sky was full of wonders.

As far as Tom could see in every direction, a strange and beautiful world was being revealed to them, a world of hot, fiery landscapes, towering ice mountains, swirling gas clouds and yellowy seas.

Moving over and under and through this world, an infinite variety of strange and beautiful creatures paraded themselves, some with luminous heads, others with watery tentacles a thousand miles long or eyes bulging on the end of long, curling stalks. Yet more appeared to have superhuman powers, walking on water, changing shape and colour, becoming invisible and communicating in languages too complex for human beings to understand. The sky pulsated as one fantastic image followed another until, suddenly, it turned flame-red and seven huge black moons appeared across it. Calypso pointed upwards and, to everyone's delight, spoke her first word:

'Laybud.'

Ladybird. Tom laughed. Of course. Now he understood why some of the images felt strangely familiar. The Fizzle had played one last trick on them, taking them through the tunnel not to show them the wonders of another world, but to show them the magic of their own. The red and black perfection of a ladybird's wing, the long, flowing tentacles of a river system, the mysterious unseen creatures that inhabit the earth's ocean depths. Then the ladybird was gone too, and the tour began to quicken. The world's wonders flashed across the sky faster and faster until they were almost tumbling over each other, appearing for no more than a split second before being pushed aside. Quicker still and the images started to blur together in a dizzying kaleidoscope of colour until, suddenly, as the air cracked like thunder around them, they merged together as one, in a single blinding white flash. The show was over.

But no one moved. Instead, around the world – from the street markets of Shipley to the bazaars of Baghdad – its people, awestruck by what they had just seen, continued to stare up at the sky, their mouths gaped open in wonder like hungry young birds waiting to be fed. And fed they were. As the cloud screen began slowly to return to its natural silvery state, so it started to dissolve until, finally, the Fizzle fell as rain on to a billion waiting tongues.

Voices

'Is Scarlett with you?' asked Hopper.

'She's sitting in the co-pilot's seat next to me,' Tom replied, 'unwrapping a toffee.'

Hopper chuckled. 'That'll be for you. She knows I could never take off without one. And she doesn't mind us borrowing her seaplane?'

'Of course not. But she's a little worried the excitement might be too much for you.'

'Humbug! Tell that great granddaughter of mine that I want you to make this flight a real scorcher. Loop the loops, barrel rolls, spins and dives, leave nothing out. I want to feel what it's like to be the best aerial gymnast in the squadron again.'

'I'll do my best,' Tom promised, 'or rather, *your* best.'

He pulled Hopper's battered old flying goggles down over his eyes.

'Are you relaxed enough to start our pre-flight checks?' he asked.

'I'm in bed too weak to lift so much as a little finger,' Hopper reminded him. 'How much more relaxed could I be? Now get a move on, old chap. I may be a hundred and six years old but I still have things to do.'

Tom laughed.

'In that case . . . can you feel the plane's joystick in my hands?' he asked.

'Check,' Hopper replied, confidently.

'And the rudder pedals under my feet?'

'Check. I can even hear them squeaking when you press them.'

'And my view from the cockpit, can you see that too?' Tom continued, taking the toffee from Scarlett.

'Check,' Hopper replied. 'What a glorious sunset – and all the better for seeing it through my old goggles.'

Tom nodded to Scarlett. Everything was ready. From the quiet stillness of his room Hopper had stepped into Tom's mind as though it were a perfectly fitting suit, so that he could see and hear and feel everything that Tom could. And Tom wasn't about to disappoint him. As the new custodian of Hopper's flying skills he was determined to give their true owner the ride of his life. He popped the toffee into his mouth, and with a final wave to Polly, and Pepe, and Paco, and Moolah, and all the other shipmates who had gathered on the Crow's Nest to watch, he brought the seaplane's powerful engine roaring into life. As it gathered speed the plane began skimming lightly over the sparkling amber sea like a perfectly thrown pebble until, finally, Tom pulled hard on the joystick and Hopper Hawkins, his mission accomplished, rose into the sky for the last time.

Acknowledgements

My thanks go to Jo, Jessica, Sarah and Samuel and the many friends and family who have helped Shipley Manor on its maiden voyage.